CUBAN CRIME OF PASSION

A JAKE SULLIVAN NOVEL

CHIP BELL

THE JAKE SULLIVAN SERIES

Come Monday

Trying to Reason with Hurricane Season

Havana Daydreamin'

A Pirate Looks at Forty

One Particular Harbour

Son of a Son of a Sailor

Jamaica Mistaica

Changes in Latitudes, Changes in Attitudes

He Went to Paris

Tampico Trauma

Fins

Big Rig

We Are The People Our Parents Warned Us About

Cuban Crime of Passion

ALSO AVAILABLE:

Trilogy

The First Ten Adventures

COMING FALL 2019:

Gypsies In The Palace

CUBAN CRIME OF PASSION

A JAKE SULLIVAN NOVEL

CHIP BELL

Printed in the United States of America.

"It's just a Cuban crime of passion,
Messy and old fashioned.
Yeah, that's what the papers did say.
It's just a Cuban crime of passion,
Anejo and knives a slashin'."

– "CUBAN CRIME OF PASSION"
BY JIMMY BUFFETT

Dedication

To Michael J. Langer, a/k/a Mike Lang, my best friend for a quarter century, who is celebrating his 60th spin around the sun. This one is yours!

Acknowledgement

To Eve, who continues putting up with me as I continue to write these novels, and to all those who continue to read them.

A special thanks to all those folks in the Trop Rock/Tropical Americana Universe for supporting the Jake Sullivan Series. I started writing because I thought it would be fun, and it certainly has been, but my interactions with the singers, songwriters, broadcasters, and fans of Trop Rock has made it so much more.

I also want to especially acknowledge Maria Elena Taylor, a wonderful young lady I met at last year's MOTM, who told me a fascinating story that has become a part of this book. This is the best part of what I do – meeting so many wonderful people who tell me such interesting things and make my job so very enjoyable.

PROLOGUE

CHAPTER 1

The applause was loud and prolonged at the board meeting held at the Angelena Caroselli Children's Memorial Hospital in Havana, Cuba.

A tall man with a stern visage, the newly elected Chairman of the Board, slowly stood and thanked the members.

"I want to thank you for your votes of confidence in Grupo Cuarecin. Together, we'll take the necessary steps to make the eradication of childhood disease a reality."

He reached for the teak cane with solid gold handle that laid on the table before him, his left arm hanging limply by his side, and walked slowly to the door, a wry smile on his face, as the group once again burst into applause.

"*You better clap loudly and long*," thought Anthony Ritzo. "*My ten million dollar gift is worth at least that to you fools. How surprised you would be if you knew what your new lab, earmarked for biotechnical studies, investigation, and experimentation, really would produce.*"

CHAPTER 2

An encrypted phone sent a signal bouncing off several towers around the world, and a phone rang in a small, neat house with a carefully tended garden, in which sat a stone fountain, in the Siboney area outside of Havana.

"Funny you should call," said the old man. "I am in my garden looking at my fountain. I assume, given your friend's condition, there is trouble. You know, I will gladly help, but I must tell you . . . your help is needed here. Let us make our arrangements."

THE FRIEND

CHAPTER 3

An old man drove his white 1954 Mercury Monterrey down a side street in the Siboney District, outside of Havana, and parked it in front of his favorite barista. He looked into the sky. The morning was bright and clear.

"*A good omen*," he thought.

As he entered, he looked around and found the man he was looking for and acknowledged his friend with a wave and a smile. Together they walked through the small café and exited through a back door, where a beat up blue pickup truck sat with the engine running.

They exchanged the light jackets they were wearing, and a fedora was exchanged for a baseball cap, and the old man got into the pickup truck and drove away, while the other man returned for his morning coffee and paper, sitting by a window where he could be observed. But, more importantly, where he could also see those observing him.

CHAPTER 4

A twin engine Sportcraft, flying the flag of Canada, cut its engines as it pulled into the harbor of Mariel, approximately forty miles west of Havana.

A man with a sandy beard adjusted his cap, lifted a small duffle bag, and stepped up onto the dock after securing his lines.

He was met by two Cuban Federales and offered his papers. A Canadian Passport was produced, the bag was checked, and Mr. Steven Byers made his way to a parking lot where a blue pickup truck honked its horn. Byers headed in its direction and stooped to look into the driver's side window, where he was greeted by the beaming smile of Silvio Caroselli.

"Welcome to Cuba, Mr. Byers."

Mr. Byers walked around the back of the vehicle and opened the passenger door, tossed his duffle behind the seat, smiled broadly, and extended his hand to the man behind the wheel.

"Good to see you, Silvio. After all this time, I think you can call me Mike."

CHAPTER 5

"What happened to the Mercury?"

"A friend has it at the moment. I decided it would be best if I was less conspicuous, and I apologize for the mode of transportation, Mr. Lang."

"Silvio, please, call me Mike!"

"Very well, Mike. I am so glad to see you after these several years. Please, I read so much in the papers. How is Mr. Sullivan doing?"

Mike thought about the last time he had seen Jake lying in a hospital bed, unconscious, showing no spontaneity, little movement except for reflexes, not knowing what his future would be.

"Not well, Silvio, I'm afraid the gunshot wound did some damage to his brain and caused a lot of swelling. All we can do is wait."

"I am so sorry," said Silvio. "He's a good man," and then looking at Mike, "you both are."

"Thank you, Silvio."

"I have been praying for him, and I will continue to."

Mike nodded, looking at the old man who had once been in Meyer Lansky's crime family, but always a devout

Catholic, and as Mike found out, a good and honest man, principled in his own way and with his own sense of justice.

"Silvio, we're in this truck because you're trying to avoid someone or something. You told me on the phone that you needed my help. What's going on?"

"It's complicated. Let's wait until we get to my home and we can discuss it further. And, you have come here, obviously, about Mr. Sullivan. How can I help you?"

"There's not much you can do, Silvio. I'm here for the man who did this to Jake. Except for a place to sleep and a few other things I might need, I don't intend to involve you or anyone else in it. This is something I'm going to do, and make no mistake about it, I *am* going to do it."

"I understand how you feel, Mr. Lang. When I was young, I had to do things . . . sometimes for revenge, sometimes it was only business . . . but whatever the reason, killing stays with you, of that there is no doubt."

CHAPTER 6

There was silence on the way to Silvio's house, except for a smattering of small talk.

When they entered, Mike felt as if he were back in time . . . the house looked exactly the same. The old man sat in an overstuffed chair and sighed.

"Silvio, you said you needed help. What's the problem?"

"The lab at the hospital. Children are dying. Quick cremations. We are told that it is due to an onslaught of infectious diseases . . . but there are supplies moving in and out at night. I still have friends there, and I'm trying to find out what's going on."

"I don't understand," said Mike, "the hospital was built in honor of your daughter. It was one of the best things that was done here. Instead of leaving Cuba, doctors are coming back, especially those who treat children's diseases."

Silvio shook his head.

"I know. And for quite a while, that's the way things were working . . . but then the new group took over."

CHAPTER 7

"What new group?" asked Mike.

"It's a conglomerate. I don't exactly know," said Silvio, "it's like a spider with a very large web. Its name is 'Grupo Cuarecin'. It owns a lot of things and is making inroads all over the island. The main man is Anthony Ritzo. Very rich. Very mysterious. He gave the hospital ten million dollars for a new laboratory. They named him Chairman of the Board. This hospital was built in memory of my daughter, Angelena, and I can't sit back and let it be destroyed by these people. I know something's wrong, and I have to find it . . . and . . . I was hoping you could help."

CHAPTER 8

Mike looked at the old man and remembered how he had been beaten because he had dared to help them when he and Jake had gone after missing mob money in Cuba. He was their friend. He sighed and nodded. His revenge would have to wait.

The old man smiled and slapped the arms of his chair as he rose up, knowing he had gained an ally.

"Thank you, Mr. Lang! Thank you! And do not worry. While you are helping me, I will be helping you. In fact, I have already begun. But for now . . . come . . . put your things in your room, wash up after your long trip, and there is food and drink waiting for you in the kitchen. I must leave and make some plans, but I will be back shortly," and he held out his hand. Mike took it, and Silvio pulled him close and hugged him and then stepped back.

"Enough. I must go."

CHAPTER 9

Pulling the ball cap lower on his head and smiling, Silvio was out the door. Mike heard the engine of the truck and watched through the window as the blue jalopy backed out onto the road, and then he was gone.

Mike walked back to the bedroom, made some calls on his encrypted phone. As he did every day, he checked on Jake. There was some movement – probably only reflexive – no further change, after it was determined he could at least breathe on his own. Mike ended the call and sighed.

"*Would he ever recover? My best friend. Or would this be his condition until the end?*"

Then his countenance changed. Feeling pity for Jake or for himself would do no good. Jake was a fighter, and he would make it back. Mike had to focus on the task at hand. He would help Silvio, but he had to remember that he was there for one purpose and one purpose only . . . to kill the man responsible, the Leader of Group 45, and kill him he would.

CHAPTER 10

It was almost evening when Silvio arrived back at his house. Mike was sitting at the kitchen table, eating one of the pulled pork sandwiches Silvio had left for him and drinking a Cristal beer.

Silvio took off the cap and made his way back to the kitchen.

"Ahh, I see you found the food and drink. I hope it is to your liking."

"Everything is great, Silvio. Thank you. I appreciate it. I'm sorry to disrupt your house."

Silvio waved his hands as if to encompass his entire home.

"Mr. Lang, it is not much, but it is my home. It was where my wife and child and I had many happy moments, but I am an old man and the place is now quiet. Believe me, I enjoy your company more than you know."

"Well, Silvio, I'm glad to be here. It's good to spend time with an old friend."

Silvio chuckled as he made his way to the ice box and took out another sandwich.

"You heated this?" he asked Mike.

"I did. Managed to do it without blowing up the microwave."

"Yes, the microwave. One of the hallmarks of progress here in Cuba," and he chuckled again as he warmed up the sandwich and opened a Cristal for himself. After the microwave dinged, Silvio took his sandwich and beer to the kitchen table and sat opposite Mike and began to eat.

"Finish your sandwich, and then I will take you to El Escondite."

"To where?" asked Mike.

Silvio winked at him and said, "The Hideout, of course."

THE HIDEOUT

CHAPTER 11

After a half hour of driving west from Siboney, they came to a track that went off to the right and Silvio took it. It was dark, and his headlights picked up scrub along both sides of the road, with a faint glow in the distance.

As they proceeded, the faint glow became windows in a small ramshackle building with a weathered sign that said *El Escondite.*

"What is this place?" Mike asked Silvio as Silvio cut the engine and began to exit.

"Come, come. You'll meet my friend, Tony, and we will make sure you are properly attired."

Mike had on a pair of jeans and a polo shirt.

"What's wrong with the clothes I'm wearing?"

"You will see, Mr. Lang. You will see," as Silvio rushed ahead of him and opened the door.

Before Mike entered, he heard him say, "Tony! My friend! Good to see you!"

Mike entered what was actually a small bar with four stools and a table off in the corner. It reminded him of a much more dilapidated version of the Chart Room in Key West, and behind the bar stood a man with curly gray hair, staring past Silvio, who was seated at one of the stools, directly at Mike, drying a glass. Mike felt like the hired gun in an old western until Tony Perelli put the glass on the bar and made a slight bow of his head.

"Welcome to El Escondite, Mr. Lang," he said as he came around the bar and extended his hand. Mike shook it and they exchanged smiles. "Any friend of Silvio's is a friend of mine."

CHAPTER 12

Mike looked at Silvio.

"I'm still at a loss about the 'properly attired' comment, Silvio."

"Ahh, yes . . . Tony . . . you think you can help our friend?"

"I think so. Follow me, Mr. Lang."

And with that, he walked over and moved the table slightly out of the corner, reached into his pocket, and pulled out a small remote and aimed it at the wall, which slowly slid back, revealing what appeared to be a metal door with a keypad beside it. Perelli punched in a number and then opened that door and hit a switch. Mike looked inside and then turned and looked at Silvio.

"See anything you like?"

Mike turned back and looked at what was a small armory full of all types of weaponry. Tony went inside and brought out a case.

"I think I know your weapon of choice, Mr. Lang," and he opened a case revealing a Gen 5 Glock 19."

"You have good taste, Mr. Perelli."

"This is what I use, myself."

Mike put in a clip and examined the weapon.

"It will certainly do," he said.

"Good. Now, you are properly attired," said Silvio. "Come, let's have a beer to celebrate," and they both took a seat at the bar while Tony went behind and opened three cans of Cristal. Perelli raised his beer in a toast.

"To good, safe hunting for all concerned."

Mike and Silvio joined in the toast and then each took a drink from their cans, which were ice cold. Mike looked at both Tony and Silvio with a sense of curiosity.

"I take it you two know each other?"

"You can say that," said Perelli. "We go way back. Silvio and I grew up together on the Lower East Side. Did Vegas together and came to Havana together. We both found good women . . ." and he paused, his eyes going to the ceiling as he crossed himself, "may God rest their souls. And we stayed here. At one point, there were a lot of us. This was the place where we all met and talked about old times, as old men tend to do. There aren't many of us left, are there Silvio?"

"I'm afraid not, my friend."

"Anyway, there are times when we have to do certain things and take certain actions and help certain people . . . so we sort of have our own little network of those of us who are left, to ensure our community's safety. And," he went on, "now that you're here, you are part of that community as far as we're concerned. I know why you're here, Mr. Lang, and I respect what you're doing. I also appreciate you trying to help Silvio. That hospital means everything to him, and there's something wrong. There's some bad people involved. I can feel it in my gut. And I'm here to help him and you in any way I can."

CHAPTER 13

This time Mike raised his can of Cristal.

"To old friends and new friends. I already promised Silvio I would help him, and I appreciate your offer of help, and I accept it, as far as doing whatever needs to be done to solve Silvio's problem . . . but mine is far too dangerous, and I can't ask anybody to join me in that. That one's on me, and me alone."

Perelli stared at him for a little while and then nodded his head.

"As you wish."

"Well," said Silvio, "I for one have had enough beer and am ready to retire for the evening. We have a big day ahead of us, Mr. Lang."

"Silvio, will you please call me Mike?"

"Sorry. We have a big day ahead of us, Mike."

"And why is that?" asked Mike.

"I made arrangements to meet with my friend, Jorge Tecona. He is a member of the Board of the hospital, and he has been my friend for many years. I went to see him after I left the house today, and he has agreed to meet with me and a friend of mine from Canada, a wealthy friend who might be interested in making a small donation to the hospital . . . Steven Byers . . . and Mr. Byers and I are meeting with Mr. Tecona at 9:00 A.M., tomorrow morning. So, I think we should get some rest, don't you?"

"You're driving," said Mike, as he finished his beer, stood up, and extended his hand once again to Perelli. "Thank you Tony. I appreciate everything."

"I'm here if you need anything else," he said, handing Mike a bag. "Some extra clips in there."

"How do I, ah . . ."

"No need. Your money's not good here."

Mike looked at Silvio, who just shrugged.

"Again, my thanks."

"Good hunting, Mr. Lang. Be careful. I think these guys who are trying to take over the hospital are a bad crew."

"We'll find out," said Mike.

"And I'm sure it's the same for those you are hunting."

Mike stopped at the door and turned around and nodded his head slightly.

"You have no idea," and he followed Silvio outside, where he said, "Follow me around back."

Mike did so and found himself in a gravel lot where Silvio's white 1954 Mercury Monterrey was parked. Silvio patted the hood as he walked around the car, opened the driver side door, got in, and turned the ignition key, the engine igniting immediately.

"So Tony was you this morning?" asked Mike.

"Can't be too cautious!" Silvio replied, as he took off the ball cap and replaced it with his favorite straw fedora that Tony had left in the car. "Let's go home!"

CHAPTER 14

The ride back to Silvio's home was quiet. It was a warm night and they had the windows down. The nighttime sounds of animals and plants rustling in the breeze were the only things that interrupted that silence. Finally, Silvio spoke.

"You know, I always admired Mr. Lansky and the idea he had for this place, but as I've gotten older I realize . . . had he succeeded, it would have been built on blood and the backs of the Cuban people. Probably would not have been much different than Castro, Batista, and all the rest. Such a beautiful country and beautiful people. I think that's why it bothers me so much. Now, with the new relationship with the United States, they have a chance to become free and to live and prosper on this beautiful island," and then he looked at Mike. "But the trouble is, the bad men never stop coming."

Mike looked at Silvio and then out the window, and then straight ahead.

"They never will, Silvio. The bad men always keep coming." And then he looked at Silvio in the dim light of the dashboard. “And that’s why there have to be people who stop them.”

Silvio nodded as he headed home.

THE BOARD MEMBER

CHAPTER 15

Prior to going to sleep, Mike and Silvio had concocted a plan and Silvio had written a letter he carried with him as they arrived at the hospital on the outskirts of Havana.

As Silvio pulled into the parking lot, Mike noticed the cameras on the light poles.

They entered through the main doors into the beautifully appointed lobby, and Mike's senses continued to be on alert, and he noticed how the man sitting in one of the armchairs in the waiting area shifted in his seat and moved the newspaper away to catch a glimpse of him as they entered before quickly putting it back in place. One of the custodians moved his hand ever so slightly to something lying on the top of his cart.

As they rode the elevator up to the conference room on the fourth floor and exited, they passed an electrician on a ladder, diligently working on one of the overhead lights. But as soon as they passed, Mike quickly looked back and the electrician was no longer concentrating on his work, but concentrating on them.

"I think you're right, Silvio," Mike whispered. "There's something going on here. There's an awful lot of surveillance for a children's hospital."

Silvio opened the door of the conference room, took off his fedora, peeked inside, and then entered, smiling and holding his hands out as a white-haired, well-suited man rose from the far end and strode to greet him in a warm embrace.

"Silvio, how are you, my old friend?"

"I am well, Jorge, I am well. Thank you so much. And you?"

"I have no complaints. We are still here."

"A good thing, yes?"

"Indeed."

Tecona looked past Silvio.

"And who might this be?"

"This is a friend of mine, Mr. Steven Byers, from Ottawa, Canada. He, too, lost his child to disease, and he heard about our hospital and thought perhaps he could invest some of his ill-gotten wealth with us."

"Ill-gotten?" asked Tecona.

Mike held out his hand.

"Mr. Tecona, thanks for meeting with us. Steve Byers. You have to excuse Silvio. He and I have this back-and-forth that some people just don't understand. I assure you, I made my money in the technology field and it was all properly earned, but, as I think Silvio could attest to, it didn't matter how much money I had . . . it couldn't save my little boy."

"I am sorry, Mr. Byers, for your loss. Losing a child is a horrible thing. But surely there are places in Canada where you could invest your money trying to cure childhood diseases."

"True, but I read Silvio's story about how this hospital came to be, and I started corresponding with him. I don't know. I felt sort of a kindred relationship . . . because of what happened with his daughter, I guess, and we became friends. I decided if I was going to do this, I'd rather do it where I have a friend, rather than strangers."

"Well, we are honored. Silvio is a very good man and very dear to us here at the hospital. Now, please, sit . . . and let's further discuss what it is you'd like to do."

"Well, I have about five million dollars that I'd like to put forward to help eradicate leukemia, if possible. That's what took my little boy, Tommy, and I wanted to see if that could be of some advantage to you here."

"Five million dollars – of course, of course it could. May I ask . . . did your wife accompany you on your trip?"

Mike took on a saddened expression.

"No. When we lost Tommy, it ended our marriage, also. My wife just couldn't go on. She was despondent and suffered a complete breakdown. It was a horrible thing. My family was ruined by this. It's just me right now."

"Again, my sympathies and my apologies, Mr. Byers. I would be happy to make the arrangements for such a wonderful gift to our facility."

"I do have some questions, if you don't mind."

"Of course."

"I know you just received a large sum of money from someone else. Are you sure that my money will be put to good use here?"

"Oh, you mean the money we received from Grupo Cuarecin?"

"Yes, yes, I believe that was it."

"No, I can assure you, that was merely to refurbish our laboratory. There is much more that needs to be done, and your donation would certainly be a wonderful assist to the projects we have going on in that laboratory and elsewhere in the hospital."

Silvio spoke up.

"Jorge, I told Steve about the sudden rash of infectious diseases leading to death we've had here at the hospital recently. I think he has some concerns about that."

Jorge looked sternly at Silvio.

"Silvio, you know those stories are overblown. At any hospital, there are fatalities. Unfortunately, children come here with end stage diseases, for diseases for which we yet have no cure, and yes, there are fatalities, but nothing out of the ordinary, I assure you. And I don't mean this the way it sounds, but actually, those fatalities are giving us information we need to hopefully find a cure for those problems that have led to the deaths of these sweet, innocent children."

"So, you're satisfied with your new Chairman of the Board and the direction in which this hospital is going?"

"I am," said Tecona. "Mr. Ritzo, he, umm, is an austere man, I think is the best way to describe him. He does not wear his emotions on his sleeve, but I have to believe, given his gift and his interest in the hospital, that he is doing this for its best interests."

"I'm sorry," said Mike, "I sense that you have some reservations . . . ?"

"No, he is just an aloof person is the best way to describe it. I don't doubt his compassion. I don't doubt his desire to help the children here and elsewhere with his amazing gift. But he doesn't become very emotionally involved at our meetings. He's somewhat distant."

"Well, that in and of itself isn't a bad thing," said Silvio. "Sometimes it's hard for people to deal with the deaths of children and diseases of children and the things that hurt them."

"I think that's more the situation," said Tecona. "I don't know. Perhaps it's because he has suffered, himself."

"What do you mean?" asked Mike.

"Well, he has a bad leg that requires the use of a cane, his left arm appears to be useless since he does everything with his right hand, and the left just seems to hang by his side."

Mike sat back in his chair and stared past Tecona at one of the paintings on the wall. An ocean scene with a sailboat, drifting past the setting sun. Silvio looked at him and knew that something was wrong.

"Mr. Byers," said Tecona, "Mr. Byers . . . are you all right?"

Mike looked at him.

"I'm sorry. I guess this is too much for me at the moment. I was thinking about my son. I'm not sure what to do."

Silvio spoke up again.

"Steve, take your time. I'm sure Mr. Tecona understands."

"Absolutely, Mr. Byers. Absolutely. I'm not trying to pressure you into anything. Please don't assume that I was."

"No, no," said Mike, rubbing his forehead, "I understand. It's just sometimes this becomes very hard for me to deal with."

"Jorge, would you mind if we gave Steve some time to think and we scheduled another meeting?"

"No, not at all, Silvio. That would be fine."

"Come on, Steve. We'll go and you can think things over, and whatever you decide, I'll call Jorge and we'll set up another meeting to discuss it."

"Yes. I think that would be good, Silvio. Yes. I apologize for taking up your time, Mr. Tecona. Hopefully, we'll still be able to reach an agreement."

Tecona got up and came around and shook his hand.

"I hope so, Mr. Byers. Obviously, we would appreciate the funding. And I hope it would be something that would help you get over the loss you've sustained, if that is possible."

Mike just shook his head.

"Thank you."

"Oh," said Silvio, "before we leave . . . Jorge, would you mind giving this to Mr. Ritzo?" and he handed him a letter. "I know that he doesn't know me, but given what this hospital means to me, I just wanted to personally thank him for his generous donation to the laboratory."

"I would be happy to, Silvio. As a matter of fact, we have a special Board meeting tomorrow, and I will give him your letter. You know, it is one of his quirks. Even though I am the Secretary of the Board, he prefers that I take no minutes or anything in writing while we have meetings, but I don't think this will be a problem. I'll be happy to give it to him."

"Well, if he doesn't want to keep it, just give it back to me and let me know that he's read it, and I'll just keep it."

When they got back to the car, Silvio looked at Mike, who still had a far-away look in his eyes.

"Mike, what is it?"

As if coming out of a trance, Mike focused and his resolve overtook him.

"The man who shot Jake had a limp, and I wounded him in his left arm, Silvio. The man I'm after . . . using something as good as the hospital to commit acts of great evil is the way he operates. I think your Chairman of the Board and the man I am after are one and the same!"

THE
TECHNOLO
GIST

CHAPTER 16

When Mike and Silvio got back to the house, Mike placed a call on his encrypted phone to a number in Key West. It was picked up on the second ring.

"Mr. Lang . . . are you alright?" said Sam Walsh.

"Sam, I have to tell you, this call is off the books, and there can be no evidence of it or of anything else you and I do. Sorry friend. Do you understand?"

"I do."

"And, if you don't want to do this, I perfectly understand. So, now's the time for you to decide."

"There's no decision to be made, Mr. Lang. I know what you're doing, and I know why, and I'll do anything I can to help you."

"Thanks, Sam. I appreciate it. I need you to do a deep dive into a conglomerate called Grupo Cuarecin and its head honcho, a man named Anthony Ritzo. I think he's the guy I'm after, posing as a corporate big shot. He's taken a position as Chairman of the Board of the children's hospital here in Havana. He donated ten million dollars to redo the laboratory, and I have to get proof it's him and find out what he's up to. You know, from the day I first met Ortiz in

Montana, there was something off about him. He seemed too subservient. I mean, he was evil, pure evil, but I didn't sense him as the leader type. Sometimes I think I'm wrong about him being the leader of Group 45."

"But you saw him in Key West, Mr. Lang."

"I know, but it was dark and rainy, and it was at a distance."

"And then there was the situation with Jake."

"I don't know, Sam. My gut tells me I'm right, but . . ."

"Then believe it," said Walsh. "It's served you well over the years."

"You're right, but, at any rate, we're still going to try to prove it, and here's what I plan to do," and then Mike explained about Silvio and his letter.

"If he touches it and we can get that letter back, we can get his DNA, and we'll get it sent out to the mail drop we have in Key West. If it comes in, as soon as you can, analyze it and let me know what you've found. Check it against all criminal records you can get to in Cuba and elsewhere. I want to find out who this guy really is, and hopefully, that will give me some information as to how I can stop him."

"No problem, Mr. Lang. I'm on it."

CHAPTER 17

After Mike ended his call with Walsh, he found Silvio sitting in the kitchen.

"Did your call go well?" he asked.

"Yeah. We have a good guy in Key West. Great with computers and anything technical. Anything out there that can be found, he'll find it."

Silvio looked dejected.

"And all we can do here is sit and wait to hopefully get the letter back so we can get it to him."

"No, there's something else we need to do, Silvio."

"Which is?"

"We need to get into that lab."

"That's an impossibility," said Silvio, shaking his head in a negative. "Only the director can get in. That's one of the things that bothered me, that made me suspicious. There's one of those things that you put your eye up to, and that's what unlocks the door."

"Why would you have that on a lab in a children's hospital? You mean a retinal scanner?"

"Yes. I think that is what it's called."

"How'd you find out about that?"

"One of my many godchildren on this island is a young girl named Maria Elena Taylor, and she is the chief lab assistant. She is of Cuban ancestry but was born and went to college somewhere near Tampa and then after she got her degree she decided to come to Cuba. She's a wonderful young girl. She loves kids. So, I put in a word for her and she got in as a lab assistant here and worked her way up to the chief assistant to the director."

"Perfect. She's someone who should be able to get us into the lab."

"I don't know, Mr. Lang. I don't know about this."

"What's wrong, Silvio?"

"If you're right about who these people are, we could be putting her in great danger."

"Look, so far, no one even knows I'm here, and we're going to keep it that way. You think you can come up with a reason for her to come here to visit you?"

"Absolutely," said Silvio, his mood changing and his expression swelling with pride. "Ever since she was a little girl, she loves my spaghetti and meatballs, the old Italian recipe. I can invite her for dinner."

"Done," said Mike. "Listen, we're only going to talk to her, and if she doesn't want to become involved, that's perfectly fine, we'll find another way. We'll make sure she understands the risks, and I promise you, I'll protect her."

Silvio looked disturbed and Mike understood why.

"Silvio, I promise you, this will not be Paula again."

"Very well," said Silvio, "We must go to the hospital to see if we can catch a glimpse of Mr. Ritzo, to see if you recognize him. You will take the truck, and I will drive the Mercury. The special Board Meeting is tomorrow, and if you arrive early, you may catch a glimpse of him entering the building. Meanwhile, I will go to have lunch at the hospital cafeteria tomorrow. She usually eats there. We will have a chance meeting. I'll say something about the horrible food and invite her to a lovely dinner. But, you have to promise me, Mike, not to put her in harm's way."

"I promise you, Silvio, she will be safe. I won't let it happen again."

"I believe you, Mike, and I thank you. I'm going out to the garden for a while. I need to sit on a chair under the sun and relax. You're welcome to join me."

"No. I'm going to make some calls. I want to check on Jake."

"And, also, perhaps the young lady you're seeing?"

"How'd you know about that?"

"I always keep track of my friends, Mike . . . always."

Mike just laughed.

"I bet you do."

"Please say hello to Miss Charlotte for me, if you would."

"I'll do that."

Mike went to make his calls and Silvio went outside, but he couldn't relax, and he couldn't enjoy the sun. All he could do was think of another young girl, a young girl named Paula, and the worries he had already for Maria Elena.

THE LAB ASSISTANT

CHAPTER 18

Silvio Caroselli was sitting on a plastic chair at a plastic table in the spacious cafeteria in the hospital's most lower level, playing with a piece of meat that he couldn't quite identify, that he had taken by choice to comment on later.

When he saw Maria Elena Taylor place her tray down at another table, he put on his hat and picked up the debris around him and made his way to deposit what was left of his meal in the trash and took a route to be directly in the sightline of Maria Elena.

"Silvio! My goodness, it's been so long. How are you?" she said, rising and embracing him, causing him to set his tray down on her table.

"My lovely Maria Elena. How are you, sweetheart?"

"I'm good. What brings you to the hospital?"

"Oh, you know me. I just like to stop by and check on things. I'm an old man. I don't have a lot to do."

She playfully slapped him on the arm.

"You're not old. Look at you. You're in great shape."

"Thank you, my dear, but years don't lie. I didn't mean to interrupt your lunch. I'm sorry."

"No, no. Please sit. I haven't talked to you in so long."

Silvio thanked her and took a seat. She looked at his tray and laughed.

"I see you really didn't enjoy the 'mystery meat' of the day."

"No, can't say as I did. I'm an old Italian. I need spices, seasoning. I don't think this thing was even touched by salt or pepper."

Maria Elena laughed.

"I know. I usually stick to the salad. Most of the time, at least, it's fresh."

"I'll tell you what. I really do have to go, but why don't you come over to the house? I'll make you a big platter of spaghetti and meatballs with some fresh garlic bread and a salad made right from my garden."

"You're still growing tomatoes?"

"Tomatoes and everything else."

She thought for a minute.

"I'd like that. I really would."

"Tomorrow?"

"Sure, why not."

"How about around 6:00 o'clock?"

"Mr. Caroselli, you and I have a date."

"And I am honored, young lady," he said, bowing and sweeping his fedora before him.

They both laughed, and he kissed her on the cheek.

"I'm so glad I ran into you, honey. I can't wait to just sit and talk. I'll see you tomorrow."

"Make lots of spaghetti and meatballs. You know how I love it."

"Don't worry. No one leaves Silvio Caroselli's house hungry."

They laughed again and she kissed him goodbye, and he made his way to the exit.

CHAPTER 19

Mike had done as Silvio suggested and had left early in the morning in the pickup truck and found a place in the parking lot in the shade of a palm tree, where he had a sightline of the main entrance.

Silvio had contacted Tony the night before, and when Mike arose, there was a new digital camera sitting by the keys to the pickup truck on the stand by the door.

It was close to 9:00 when a brand new Mercedes pulled into the lot and stopped outside of the main entrance. Men immediately existed the vehicle and took up positions, obviously looking for anyone who shouldn't be there and guarding a very important passenger.

Mike began taking shots and as luck would have it, when that passenger emerged, he turned, his weight resting on an ornate cane, and took off his sunglasses and flicked something off the lens before putting them back on. Mike had a clear shot of his face and took it. After clicking a few more shots as the group entered the hospital, he threw the camera on the seat beside him and banged his fist on the steering wheel. It wasn't him. He realized that he was older now, but this was not the younger man he had met in

Montana, and if this man was not the Leader, the man who had shot Jake and left him for dead, Mike had no idea who he truly was.

He was so sure. How could he have been so wrong? He sat there and went over everything that had happened in his mind, and his thoughts took him back . . . back before they even knew there was a Group 45 pulling the strings of the various puppets they came in contact with. And then he thought of a man named Clark and he picked up the camera and scanned the photos he had taken and looked long and hard at Anthony Ritzo, and he realized he had something else he had to request Sam Walsh to do. He took out his encrypted phone and tapped in a number and waited to do just that.

CHAPTER 20

It just so happened that while Silvio was meeting with Maria Elena, the special meeting of the officers of the Board of Directors was being held upstairs. The business they had to discuss was about a bond issue for a new wing to be approved. When a vote had been taken and business concluded, Jorge Tecona approached Anthony Ritzo as he was about to leave.

"Mr. Ritzo, I apologize for delaying you, but would you mind reading this letter? It's from Silvio Caroselli. This hospital was named for his daughter. I think he just wanted to thank you for your generous donation, and it would mean the world to him if you read it, and perhaps put a small note on it."

Ritzo looked at the envelope with suspicion and disdain, but then realized how Tecona was observing him, and his countenance changed. His manner became ingratiating, and with difficulty, he sat back down and smiled at Tecona.

"Absolutely. I'd be happy to," and he took the letter out of its envelope and read it. He pulled a gold pen from his inside pocket and scrawled a note and handed it back to Tecona. "Please give Mr. Caroselli my best regards."

Tecona read the note, which read:

"Mr. Caroselli,

I hope someday to meet you. Thank
you for your interest, and although
I am saddened by your loss, I take
solace in the wonderful institution
created in your daughter's memory.

Anthony Ritzo"

"That's beautiful, Mr. Ritzo," said Tecona. "I can't tell you how much Silvio will appreciate this."

"I certainly hope so," said Ritzo as he rose. "It's the least I can do for a man who is so involved with this facility. Now, I must go," and his countenance changed back to a man who wasn't sure whether or not he had just done something he might regret.

CHAPTER 21

As it happened, Tecona came out into the parking lot just as Silvio was pulling out after his meeting with Maria Elena, and he called out to him.

"Silvio!"

Silvio saw him waving and put the vehicle into park as Tecona rushed up to his open driver's side window.

"The letter. I gave it to Mr. Ritzo. He wrote you a note. Perhaps I was mistaken. He does seem to have a heart, and a very generous one at that."

"Thank you, Jorge. That's good to know, and I appreciate it greatly."

"Take care, Silvio. Stop by any time. You're always welcome here."

"Thank you, Jorge, I appreciate it. You take care, also," and he put the Mercury into gear and headed home, elated that he could tell Mike two positive things had occurred that, hopefully, would help bring down a man whom Silvio doubted, contrary to Jorge's belief, had any heart at all.

THE DINNER GUEST

CHAPTER 22

When Silvio arrived home, he could see that Mike was depressed. Mike explained to him what had occurred relative to the photographs.

Silvio sat in his favorite chair and motioned for Mike to sit down on the couch across from him.

"Mike, you live in a world of shadows. People are not who they seem. Things change quickly, and all the changes that you see aren't necessarily real. I didn't mean to eavesdrop, but I overheard part of your conversation with Mr. Walsh while I was in the kitchen. You have to go with what you believe, Mike. Go with your gut, because if it's telling you you're on the right path, stick to it. The odds are, it will lead you in the right direction."

"Thank you, Silvio. I remembered some things from the past and I'm having Sam check some things. Maybe we'll get an answer, and, hopefully, we'll see whether my gut is right or wrong. Now tell me about your day."

Silvio became excited and told Mike about Maria Elena's acceptance of his dinner invitation for the following day, and also, presented the letter, which, as Mike had directed, he immediately had placed in a plastic bag and touched in as few places as possible, hoping that Ritzo's prints wouldn't be contaminated by him and Tecona.

Pursuant to the treaty, U.S. Postal facilities had been established on the island, and Silvio drove Mike to one, where he placed the package in an overnight mailing envelope with a return address Silvio had given him of an uninhabited house on a street in Siboney, and addressed it to a drop box used by the Key West office of FSI – Fletcher Security and Investigations. To anyone who checked, there was nothing about the letter that would draw their suspicions, and Mike was sure it would get out of Cuba and arrive safely at its destination.

When he was back in the car, Mike got on the encrypted phone and alerted Walsh to look for it and to immediately get whatever information he could.

CHAPTER 23

Mike spent the remainder of that day and a good part of the next on his encrypted phone talking with Walsh and checking on Jake's condition, which hadn't changed.

He was able to catch Linda, Jennifer, and Jessica at the hospital in Miami when they were visiting Jake. They seemed to think that there was some improvement in Jake's condition, although that is not what the doctor had relayed. The girls were sure that he could hear them, and they saw responses as they spoke to him.

Mike didn't want to dim their hopes and prayed that they were right, but he had his doubts.

Even though Jake and Linda had their difficulties, Mike had always loved her and the girls, and his anger and resolve to get the man who had caused this were only fueled by their conversation. He had snapped at Walsh when he had no information to offer, knowing full well that he was doing the best he could with what he had, and as he had proven time and time again, if anybody could get information, it was him.

But Mike was frustrated and impatient. He couldn't get the image of Jake lying in the rain on Mallory Square out of his mind, and he couldn't forgive himself for not being there to help his friend.

Perhaps Maria Elena would be able to help them.

At the dinner Silvio had made for himself and Mike after he had come back from the hospital, he had gone on and on about Maria Elena. She seemed like a wonderful young girl, and here he was putting her in harm's way. He had been in Cuba before, and there had been another girl, and he had lost her. No matter what, he was not going to let that happen again.

CHAPTER 24

They had agreed that Mike would stay hidden when Maria Elena arrived and Silvio would gradually explain why he had asked her to come to dinner and then introduce him. So Mike was in the back when he heard the car pull up and the knock on the door.

"Good evening, my lovely child," said Silvio.

"Hello, godfather. You look very handsome this evening."

"Thank you. On occasion, I can do well for an old man."

"You always look good to me. I can smell the spaghetti already."

"Come, come. Sit. Dinner is ready. We can talk as we eat."

Mike liked her voice. It was exuberant, young. She spoke with passion, and she was kind to Silvio. It was clear that she was close to him. But then he heard something that impressed him even more.

"Silvio, why are there only two plates? Aren't you going to have Mr. Lang eat dinner with us?"

And with that, Mike came down the hall and entered the kitchen.

"You were right, Silvio. She's a very smart young lady."

He walked over and held out his hand.

"Good evening, Miss Taylor. I'm . . ."

"I know who you are, Mr. Lang."

"You know, I've been trying to keep every person in Cuba, outside of Silvio, from knowing I'm here. Do you mind telling me how you found out?"

"I was in the parking lot getting something from my car when you left yesterday in Silvio's blue truck. It is so rare that he uses it. I was concerned, especially when I saw it was being driven by someone else, and I took a good hard look. I recognized you immediately. After all, you are famous – especially here in Cuba. Silvio is very dear to me. I paid close attention at the dedication of the hospital and was very interested in watching the famous duo of Jake Sullivan and Mike Lang during the ceremony."

"But I wasn't . . ."

"Mr. Lang, let's just say I'm very observant . . . and that man in the cap on the edge of the crowd . . . I have a good idea who that was . . . and you have my sympathies for why that is where you were."

Mike lowered his head for a moment and then looked at her.

"Thank you. You certainly do have excellent powers of observation."

"Sit, sit, Mike," said Silvio. "I'll put out another plate. It appears we have no choice," and he looked at Maria Elena, shaking his head.

CHAPTER 25

Mike was amazed over dinner how such a young lady took control of the conversation. She steered Silvio to topics that made him very happy to discuss: his garden . . . the new wing people were talking about for the hospital. And she was kind. She asked Mike about Jake and expressed her condolences and her hope for his recovery.

Finally Mike sat back in his chair, stuffed with Silvio's Italian cooking, and he looked from Silvio to Maria Elena and he laughed.

"What do you find funny, Mr. Lang," she asked.

"It's just that I'm sitting here in a little house in Cuba being fed spaghetti by someone named Caroselli and sharing it with somebody named Taylor."

"Ah," she said, "you're trying to understand my lack of a Spanish pedigree?"

"It has crossed my mind," he said.

Silvio looked at her and smiled.

"Go ahead, tell him the story. He'll appreciate it."

"A story?" asked Mike.

CHAPTER 26

"I hope I don't bore you, Mr. Lang, but this is my story. This story was told to me by my father, Alberto Taylor, Jr., when I wanted to know why we had an American last name and all my friends' last names were Spanish. The story begins with Alan Young Taylor, who was an American from Pittsboro, North Carolina. When he was eighteen, he enlisted in the Army and became associated with the volunteer group, the Rough Riders, led by Teddy Roosevelt. They were stationed in Tampa. He was sent to Cuba, where he met Maria Luisa Ynclan Alvarez. After riding with Roosevelt at San Juan Hill, he was discharged from the Army and went back to Cuba and married Maria Luisa. They had three sons together, all born in Havana. My grandfather was the youngest. The other two boys were named Ramon and Ricardo. My grandfather did not remember his father, because he was four when his father died. My grandfather then married Amelia Herrera y Sanchez, and my father, Alberto Taylor, Jr., was born. My mother was born in Havana, and they were married on August 26, 1972, in Tampa. I was born there, along with my younger sister. My dad passed away several years ago, but I learned that

Alberto Taylor had brought my family to Tampa because he had an uncle who had come to Ybor City to make cigars. I was raised in Tampa and went to the University of South Florida, where I got my degree in medicine, and after the treaty was signed, decided to come to work at this hospital that you and Mr. Sullivan so wonderfully named in honor of my godfather's little girl.

I apologize if the story was long and tedious, but I am very much a family person and I find my history unique and interesting, even though others do not."

"On the contrary," said Mike, "I found it most interesting, and it explains a lot."

"How so?" she asked.

"You had a family that did things to make your lives better, to protect the children of that family. You had a great grandfather who fought for what he believed in, and I see all those things in you. You didn't say, but where did the Maria Elena 'come from'?"

"My mother's name. She still lives in Tampa."

"And your younger sister?"

"Her name is Alicia. She's here in Cuba. She's in Cabo Corrientes on the Guanahacabibes Peninsula in Pinar del Rio Province. She's an environmentalist. That's where the protected nature reserve is."

Mike looked at Silvio with questions in his eyes.

"Mike, let me explain," and he went to the one wall of the kitchen where what appeared to be an ancient map of Cuba hung, yellowed by the years. Guanahacabibes is here, on the westernmost point."

"Yes, it's a reserve now – land that is not to be touched."

"And don't forget," said Silvio, interrupting her, "the treasure."

"Treasure?" asked Mike.

"An old foolish legend," said Maria Elena.

"Not so fast there, young lady," said Silvio. "Mr. Lang here has uncovered many a treasure himself."

"I know, Mr. Lang. I've read about your exploits. But this one is purely fiction. My sister is there because the same company that is doing such harm to our hospital is doing harm to the natural preserve created to avoid such a thing."

Mike looked at Silvio as he recognized his way to steer the conversation back to the hospital.

"She's not there because of any treasure," she said, glaring at Silvio.

"I believe you," said Mike, "but Silvio, tell me about the treasure. You know I'm interested."

"See," said Silvio.

"Go on, godfather, tell him."

Silvio sat down after giving Maria Elena and himself a glass of his homemade Italian wine from the grapes he grew in his garden from seeds sent to him from family in Italy and opened a Cristal for Mike.

"Legend has it that one of the first and most spectacular Spanish cathedrals in the New World was in Mérida, seat of the Yucatan Bishop, and the first cathedral to be finished on the mainland of the Americas, and one of only two to be entirely built during the Sixteenth Century, and had amazing treasures stored inside – a life-sized cross of the Savior in solid gold, other relics of precious metals and gems, and barrels of gold coins. The story goes that in 1642, fearing attacks by pirates, the treasures of the cathedral were to be transported to Havana to join the Spanish treasure fleets on a trip back to Spain. However, they encountered that which they were trying to avoid, and word was sent to them that there were pirates in the area, and the crew steered for the nearest landfall, at Guanahacabibes, where the treasure was off loaded and buried. The legend goes on that only one man survived by managing to get to a church in Guane, where he left documents with coordinates of the treasure site . . . a treasure site with the Crucifix of gold, barrels of jewels, and coins . . . somewhere on the peninsula and its nearby mountains. There are still treasure seekers that go to the peninsula and hunt the treasure, and there are stories of some who have come back with gold in their hands, so who really knows?" he said, looking at Maria Elena.

"*I* know," she said, "I know that Anthony Ritzo is not looking for gold. He's mining for rare ores such as cobalt and chromium, that Cuba has in abundance, that are used in industry and in making weapons, and he's doing it right next to the natural preserve. The runoffs from blasting and digging are polluting the preserve and that is why my sister is there protesting."

"You would like Alicia," laughed Silvio, looking at Mike. "She is a spitfire."

"I see it runs in the family," said Mike, drawing a smile from Maria Elena. "It's a fascinating story, Silvio, but I'm more interested in what you said about the hospital, Maria Elena."

"And why is that?"

"Because I think Anthony Ritzo may really be a man named Antonio Ortiz, the leader of a worldwide criminal syndicate, and if he has an interest in the hospital, or an interest in mining, both are for purposes to do damage not only to Cuba, but to the world in general."

Maria got up and slammed her hand on the table, leaning into Mike, and turning her head to Silvio.

"I knew there was something going on! I knew it!"

"Mr. Lang, remember . . . you promised me."

"I'm getting there, Silvio, I'm getting there. We need access to the laboratory, Maria Elena, but we don't want to put you in any danger. We want to know if you can tell us of a way we can gain access so we can find out what's going on."

Maria Elena started pacing, talking as she walked.

"Everything is a secret there, Mr. Lang. I do paperwork that's given to me by Carmine Santino, the Lab Director. Here I am, the chief lab assistant, and I'm only allowed in the office section of the lab. Everything else is blocked off. You can't see. There are steel doors between each chamber that only Santino can open. He's rarely there during the day, and there are rumors that he only appears at night. I know one thing for a fact . . . they're killing children. Children with terminal illnesses, yes, but they're speeding those illnesses along. I came in early one morning and there were guards at the doors and empty gurneys in the hallway.

I was told I couldn't enter the lab and to come back later, and I was escorted out of the hospital. There's something going on, Mr. Lang, and that something is evil."

"Can you give us any way to get in?"

"The only thing I can tell you is you're going to need Santino."

Mike looked at Silvio and thought for a moment.

"What happens if someone tries to get into the lab?"

"Everybody has a card swipe. The card swipe alerts the retinal scan. If the retinal scan isn't activated within thirty seconds, a silent alarm goes off."

"How do you know that?" asked Silvio, "if the alarm is silent?"

"I was working late in the hospital doing the paperwork that I'm allowed to do in my office, which is outside the lab. I had just turned off my light and was going to leave when the elevator doors opened and I heard a commotion. Santino was there with two armed men, complaining that his phone had received an alarm that someone had been trying to enter the lab. I don't know if someone was or it was a malfunction, but he found everything to be all right, and then he and the men left. I waited until they were gone before I left so they wouldn't see me, but I overheard their conversation."

"That's it, Silvio," said Mike. "That's how we get in. We trip the alarm, and we make Santino come to the lab, take out the guards, and make him let us in."

"I don't know, Mike."

"Silvio, I apologize. I used the wrong language. I'm used to having Jake around. That's only me doing all of the above. You will be nowhere near that hospital when all this goes down . . . and neither will you, young lady."

"But we have to swipe a card to activate the retinal scan to sound the alarm," said Silvio, "and I am not letting Maria Elena's card be used. They'll know she's in on it."

"That's true," said Mike.

"I think I can help you, there," said Maria Elena.

"You are not participating in this, young lady," said Silvio.

"No, no . . . there was another tech before me. Evidently, when she cleaned out her locker, which is now mine, she wasn't too careful and left her card swipe in it. I can give it to you and you can swipe it. There will be no connection to me or anyone else."

"What about the poor girl whose name is on it?"

"She's not even on the island. She moved back to Florida. They won't know who picked it up, where it came from, or how it got there."

"I don't know," said Silvio, "it still seems risky."

"It's our only hope, Silvio, and Maria Elena is right. She won't be tied to this."

"I don't like it, but I know we have to do it."

"Then we have a plan," said Mike. "Thank you, Maria Elena. I appreciate your courage and your honesty."

"Just get these people, Mr. Lang."

"I intend to. How soon can you get me the swipe card?"

She walked over to where her purse was sitting on the counter and opened it.

"I just never took it out," and she gave a photo I.D. card to Mike with the name of Tina Fuentes.

"Well, Tina, looks like you're our key to the lab."

THE LAB DIRECTOR

CHAPTER 27

After Maria Elena was safely on her way home and Silvio decided he was going to call it an early night, Mike went out to the garden and began work on his encrypted phone.

His first call was to Charlotte Kosior, with whom he had fallen deeply in love. She knew that he would never discuss the mission with her, but made him promise to call her to let her know that he was safe, and he made such a call.

"Well, Charlie, how are things in the world of Native American Archeology?"

Charlie, as she was called, had been named Director of Native American Antiquities by the Smithsonian, based in part upon her exploits with Jake and Mike in Montana and her skills and education and abilities with which Jake and Mike had nothing to do whatsoever.

"Are you safe?"

"I am."

"When do you think you're coming home?"

"I can't say, Charlie. I just don't know."

"I flew down to spend the weekend with Jake, today."

"Any changes?"

"The girls were there. They think so, but I couldn't see anything myself. I don't know whether it's wishful thinking on their part, or not. I just don't know, Mike."

"Well, hopefully I'll be done soon and I can start yelling at him again to get his ass out of bed."

Charlie laughed.

"If anybody can, you can."

"I don't know, Charlie. I think that's even beyond my skills. I'm good at pushing Jake's buttons, but I don't know if those buttons are even there anymore."

"Keep the faith, Mike. He's going to make it."

"I hope you're right."

"I know I can't ask you where you are or what you're doing, but I have my suspicions."

"Just leave it at that, Charlie."

"I know. I am. But I know it's dangerous. Promise to be careful . . . and promise to come home to me."

"I promise. Nothing will keep me from appearing on your doorstep."

"You better not be lying to me, Mike Lang. I love you, but if you're lying . . ."

"I'm not, Charlie. I'll be home. Now, I've got to go."

"Be careful. I love you."

"I love you, too," and he ended the call.

Next up was Sam Walsh.

"Listen, Sam, I think I've found a way to get into the hospital lab."

Walsh, having been previously briefed by Mike on the situation, asked, "What do you need me to do?"

"Get hold of Fletcher. Have him get the warrant we need for U.S. intervention on Cuban territory. I have a bad feeling as to what's in this lab and we may need a team from Guantanamo there quickly, and Fletcher's the only one who can do it."

"How long do we have?" asked Walsh.

"I'm going in tomorrow night, if everything works, I hope."

"I don't know if even Fletcher can pull that off."

"He can. I've seen him do it any number of times. Just call him and tell him to get it in the works."

"Will do."

"You have anything else for me?"

"Not yet, Mr. Lang, but I hope to shortly."

"Soon as you can, you understand?"

"Absolutely."

"All right. I'm hanging up. Call Fletcher."

CHAPTER 28

The next day no one noticed the sandy-haired man who came to the hospital in the early morning hours with a bouquet of flowers shielding his face and entered the elevator. Instead of going up, he went down as he had been directed by Maria Elena and found where the custodians' equipment and clothing were kept. Taking the clothing he needed and hoping it would fit, he left by the way he had come in.

When he came back that night after dark, he waved to the front desk, cap pulled low over his head, and took the stairs to the lowest level, where he picked up a push cart and then headed for the laboratory's floor.

Once there, he took the card he had been wearing on the lanyard around his neck, hoping that no one would notice the photograph or name, and hoping to give himself some authenticity, as he made his way through the hospital, and swiped the card. The retinal scan came to life and Mike counted down the thirty seconds until the silent alarm should have gone off, and then he moved back into the stairwell to see what would occur.

CHAPTER 29

Carmine Santino was sitting in one of Havana's better restaurants, La Mimosa, with his wife, when his cell phone began buzzing. He threw down his napkin in disgust.

"It's the lab. The alarms are going off. Something is wrong. I must go."

His wife's face was one of resignation and anger.

"Why do you work for these men? Why?"

Santino got up and moved toward his wife and clenched her jaw in his hand, holding it up to his.

"So you can enjoy dinners like this one, my dear."

He looked to the waiter.

"Please get a car for my wife."

He smiled at her and said, "Don't wait up."

"Believe me, I won't," she said, trying to pull her face away from his, but he increased the pressure.

"Remember your place, my dear, and don't interfere with my business."

He then let her go and walked away. She felt all eyes in the restaurant on her and swore that he would never do that again, her hatred growing of the man to whom she was married.

CHAPTER 30

Mike was waiting in the stairwell when Santino and two guards came out of the elevator. He waited until they had gone past him, when he silently opened the door and slid out. He had taken extra clips and a silencer from the bag Tony had given him and raised the Glock.

"Don't make a move."

The guards and Santino froze in place.

"Turn around."

All three did as directed.

"Fingertips only . . . weapons on the floor."

The guard to the right complied, but as he was kneeling down to place his weapon on the floor, the other decided it was his moment. He was wrong, as Mike put two bullets center mass, and he slid to the floor with his back against the wall of the laboratory. For some reason it made the second guard more foolish than brave, as he stopped his downward movement with the weapon and raised it toward Mike, ending up in a sitting position the same way as his friend.

Mike approached Santino, who was now trembling and sweating profusely. He spun him around to face the door and put the silenced barrel at the base of his brain.

"Open the door."

"I can't."

"Yes, you can, and if you don't, I will shoot you."

"No, you won't," stuttered Santino. "If you kill me, you can't get in."

"I didn't say I would kill you," said Mike, as he moved the muzzle of the gun to Santino's knee and pressed it as hard as he could. "But I will make sure that you never walk again."

"They'll kill me!" he shouted.

"Maybe, maybe not, but what I will do to you will be far worse!"

Santino, still trembling, needed three attempts to properly swipe his card and put his eyes to the retinal scan, but when he did, they could hear the tumblers turn and the door opened. They were in a room of computer equipment and desks, looking like a normal laboratory. Mike saw nothing out of the ordinary, but the room was too small. The lab took up the entire floor. There had to be more.

"Where's the rest of it?" he asked, again pointing the muzzle in the back of Santino's neck.

"I can't," whispered Santino, now weeping.

"Look, asshole," said Mike, "you decided to dance with the Devil . . . now you pay the price. Now, where is it?" as he lowered the gun to Santino's spine.

"This way," he said, and they moved together to a wall. Santino opened a drawer in a desk that revealed a keypad, and he punched in a code. A steel door slid back, revealing a huge room filled with row after row of test tubes, syringes, and metal cases.

"What is all this?" Mike asked. "What are you really doing here?"

Santino stuttered and cried.

"They are biological weapons we are developing."

"How many have been shipped?"

"I don't know."

Mike pushed the gun in harder at the base of his spine.

"Two. Two cases. Two cases were sent out two nights ago."

"To where? I said to where?" as Santino continued to whimper.

"Somewhere in Key West. That was the pickup point. They went by boat."

He spun Santino around and put the muzzle of the weapon under his chin.

"What type of agent was it?"

"A deadly, wind-blown Bubonic strain."

"Tell me, Santino, how'd you do tests to find out if these things worked?"

"I'm sorry!" stammered Santino. "You have to understand. I was forced to do things. They told me that the children that they brought here were near death anyway."

"So you used children as guinea pigs to develop this shit? Is that what you're telling me?"

"I didn't know . . . I didn't know . . . I'm sorry."

"You knew. You knew exactly what you were doing, you son-of-a-bitch! Tell me, you have to have a fail-safe in here if one of these tests goes bad, if you lose power or something goes sideways, you have to have a way to stop this. What is it?"

"I can't! I can't! It'll destroy everything!"

"Exactly . . . now where is it?"

Santino moved further into the room and came to a vault.

"Open it," said Mike.

He pressed another keypad and the door came open, revealing a switch.

"What's it do?"

"It's an activation device," stammered Santino. "If I hit it and shut the door, when we leave this room, the temperature will begin to drop to well below freezing and every organism will die. It cannot be opened without a special code only I have."

"So it will neutralize all of the weapons?"

"Yes. I can't. Do you know how much time and money has been put into . . ."

Mike cut him short.

"Don't talk to me about time and money! You tested these diseases, these plagues, on children," and he reached up and hit the red button and slammed shut the vault.

"No!" screamed Santino, as Mike spun him around and pushed toward the door. "We have to get out! We have to get out!"

"Why?" asked Mike.

"Because, you fool! We'll freeze to death! Don't you see what's happening here?"

Mike saw vents open, and cold air rushed into the room. The walls became coated with moisture, which Mike knew would soon turn to ice, as the temperature began to drop drastically.

"Tell me again. Tell me, Santino, what will happen?"

"We'll freeze to death!"

"Then we better get moving," and he pushed Santino further toward the door, but just as they got there, he took him by the collar and threw him backwards. The floor was now slippery and Santino skidded across and crashed into a cart, sending vials and test tubes and other glassware shattering across the floor, as he himself fell down in a heap. Mike turned and pointed the Glock at him.

"I was going to put a bullet in your brain, but you deserve a far worse death than that, and now you're going to have it," and he shut the door on Santino's screams and exited the lab. He felt no guilt, no remorse. He had rid the world of a monster, but the greater monster still lived . . . but not for long.

Mike went on his encrypted phone.

"Walsh, you got that team in place?"

"Fletcher couldn't get a warrant, Mike, not until tomorrow."

"What? You're telling me that Jordan Fletcher, the past President of the United States, couldn't get a warrant on the evidence I gave you?"

"He said the judge wouldn't do anything with an anonymous source, and he wasn't going to give you up."

"Jesus."

"I'm sorry, Mike. You're on your own."

"Well, at least I have things under control. Get it done tomorrow as fast as you can. When they get here, they're going to find an ice box with a frozen lab director inside."

"Sounds like you've been busy," said Walsh.

"Not as busy as we're going to be. This lab was created to manufacture biological weapons . . . and two cases have been shipped."

"To where?"

"Think of a small area, close to this source, with almost constant wind movement, and restricted access in and out."

"What are . . . oh no! . . . My God . . . Key West!"

"Get everyone on it . . . they went by boat two nights ago, so they're already there."

"I'm on it," and the phone wend dead.

But just then the phone buzzed again. He answered.

"Who is this?"

"Mike, it's Silvio."

"How are you calling me?"

"Don't you remember a long time ago when you left Cuba you gave me an encrypted phone in case I had to get hold of you guys? It has your number in it."

"What?" asked Mike, shaking his head.

"There are a bunch of armed men heading your way."

"How many?" asked Mike.

"A half dozen."

"All right. I'll take care of . . . how do you know this?"

"I'm in the parking lot."

"I told you to stay away from here tonight!"

"I had to. Maria Elena wouldn't listen. She was going to come on her own."

"She's with you?"

"I couldn't stop her. The least I could do was come with her and protect her."

"We'll talk about this later. Right now I have other problems," and he hung up.

"*If they were smart, they'd take the stairway and elevator*," thought Mike. "*They'll be expecting me to come down*," he thought to himself. He made his decision and entered the stairwell and headed up the stairs two at a time, already hearing noise coming from below.

Two floors up, he quietly opened the door and slid into the deserted hallway. He made his way as quickly as he could to the elevators and watched as the numbers ascended. Sure enough, it had stopped on the lab floor.

He waited until it got to his floor and the door opened, gun at the ready. It was empty. He got in and pressed down, hoping at this time of the night it would be a direct drop to the main floor, but no such luck. It stopped on the lab floor and the doors opened.

"*I'm a sitting duck here*," he thought, and rolled out onto the floor, coming up weapon at the ready. He had been right. There had been two guards posted between the entrance to the lab and the elevators – one covering the stairway and one pointing a gun directly at him.

Mike didn't hesitate taking out the gunman, aiming at him first, and then the one that turned from the stairway.

He jumped back on the elevator just as the doors were closing and exited on the main floor, walking as quickly as he could without drawing attention to himself. He exited the hospital and headed for Silvio's old pickup truck that he had used to get there. As he did, he saw the white Mercury moving toward him.

"You two obviously don't know how to listen. Now get the hell out of here! I'll meet you at the house."

Without saying a word, Silvio moved past him and out of the parking lot and headed down the street. Mike waited long enough to see the commotion inside the hospital and lights going on all over. They were hunting for him, but he was already out of the lot and on his way before the front doors even opened.

THE ASSASSIN

CHAPTER 31

Mike got to Silvio's house after he and Maria Elena had already entered. He stormed into the room.

"What the hell is wrong with you two! Do you know the danger you put yourselves in? If those cameras caught you, these people are going to tie this all together . . . and they *will* come after you!"

"We were careful, Mike. Nobody saw us."

"How do you know, Silvio?"

"Mike, I couldn't let her go."

"And you!" he said looking at Maria Elena.

"Don't lecture me Mr. Lang. I'm a big girl. I can take care of myself."

"Really? You think you can go after these people and live to tell about it?"

"You have, haven't you?"

"You have no idea what you're getting yourself into. Now, I'm calling Walsh, and I'm gathering a team from Guantanamo here tomorrow as soon as possible, and they are going to take you in and you are going to stay there until this thing is over – do you understand me!"

"You can't tell me what to do!" yelled Maria Elena.

"There's no argument about this. Do you understand me?"

"Maria Elena," said Silvio, "listen to him. He's right. We were foolish. I'm sorry, Mike."

"It's past the time for sorry, Silvio. Now, you two, get blankets and whatever will make you comfortable. You're sleeping on the floor tonight. I don't want anyone near the doors, near the windows, or above floor level."

"You think they're coming for us, don't you?" asked Silvio.

"It's a good bet."

"What are you going to do?" asked Maria Elena.

"I'm going to stand sentry to keep you protected as best I can. Now, turn out these lights and do what I told you."

"Come on, Maria Elena. Do what he says."

And they did.

CHAPTER 32

Mike had found a semi-comfortable place behind what he believed was a begonia bush. It sat off to the left by itself, and it gave him a clear view of anyone moving toward Silvio's house from three sides. There was no way he could see the fourth side, but he had to take the risk. It also gave him a view across the road. He stayed low and quiet, only rubbing his legs and arms when necessary to restore circulation in case he had to move quickly.

It was close to dawn and nothing had happened. Maybe he was wrong. Maybe they hadn't spotted Silvio and Maria Elena. Maybe everything was going to be all right . . . but he wasn't wrong.

CHAPTER 33

The man in the villa on the north shore of Cuba was furious as he listened to the report from one of his henchmen.

"We couldn't shut off the freezing unit because we didn't have the code for the lock, and by the time we broke in through the wall and crossed the wires, it was too late. Everything was destroyed, but we cleared it out – everything. There's no trace of it. Scrubbed the computers. Everything is gone, including Santino. They can't get anything on you."

"Wonderful. Millions of dollars of biological weapons destroyed . . . destroyed by *him*!" screamed the man as he limped over to the chair where his henchman was sitting and threw a photo in his face. The henchman picked it up and looked at it.

It showed a sandy-haired man getting in an old beat up pickup in the hospital parking lot.

"Who is he?"

"My God, I'm surrounded by idiots!"

One of his lieutenants snatched the picture away from the seated man.

"It's Mike Lang."

"Yes! It *is* Mike Lang . . . who, incidentally, has been in Cuba for God knows how long, doing God knows what . . . other than, of course, sabotaging my prize project. And nobody knew he was here. What do I pay you fools for?!" he screamed.

He picked up another photograph.

"And the old man . . . Silvio Caroselli. Didn't I tell you people, when I came back from Key West, to keep an eye on him because of his past relationship with Sullivan and Lang?"

"We did."

"And?"

"We've had eyes on the old Merc of his the whole time."

"And was he always in it?"

"Uh . . . ."

"As I thought. And who is she?"

"She's Santino's lab assistant."

"Really? Did you know that she's also Caroselli's goddaughter?"

"No, boss, we didn't know. I'm sorry."

"I see, well, it's good that you're sorry," he said, moving back toward his desk. He picked up something, and moving with a quickness that belied his limp, went to the seated man and shot him between the eyes. "Your apology is not accepted. Get him out of here!"

And the rest of the lieutenants scurried to remove the body.

"Santos, stay," he said. "I want our best man. We know where they are. Send him to Caroselli's house. Kill Caroselli and the girl and bring Lang to me. It's time to finish this."

"You've got it, boss."

"And . . . no mistakes."

"Understood."

"*Mistake*," thought the man, "*that letter from Caroselli. Have I made one myself?*"

CHAPTER 34

"*The sky is that strange color,*" Mike thought. "*The indigo when night changes to day, but the sun hasn't risen yet.*"

And then he spun around, weapon at the ready as he heard movement behind him. Silvio was moving toward him, crouched low with, unbelievably enough, a cup of steaming coffee in his hand.

"What are you doing?" whispered Mike, as he approached near enough to hear him.

"I thought you could use it," said Silvio.

"Doesn't anybody listen to me? This is like being with Jake. He never listens to me. Nobody listens to me."

But his thoughts became a cold calculation of necessary movement as he saw the red spot appear on the center of Silvio's chest, and he grabbed his legs, pulling them toward him, making Silvio go flat on his back, the coffee cup flying behind him. Then he heard the thunk of the bullet in the tree behind Silvio, some distance away.

"Stay here," he said to Silvio. "And please, this one time, listen to me and *do not* move!"

Mike rolled to his left, still behind the bushes, hoping that the assassin had seen only Silvio. He crawled along the perimeter of the property, keeping as low as he could, until he figured he had flanked the shooter, knowing that he would be preparing for another shot before he made a move toward the house. He crossed the road at an angle, trying to figure trajectory and where the shot had come from. The ground was wet from the morning dew, so he could tread softly, with nothing dry under his feet giving away his presence. His plan was to climb above the shooter's nest and come at him from behind.

He thought he had reached the high point and started to slowly make his way down, and then he saw him. He hadn't waited. He was moving across the road, and Mike went after him, no longer concerned about the noise, firing as he went, trying to draw his fire in return, and he got it, volley after volley, as he crashed into the stand the shooter had made, seeing the sniper weapon against the tree, knowing he had switched to an automatic for his assault on the house. And then the shooting stopped.

"*He's reloading*," he thought, and Mike started to get up to move on down the slope when he heard two more shots, but not from an automatic weapon. It was a hand gun.

He furiously headed down the slope, hitting the road at a run, praying that he wouldn't find what he knew could be a distinct possibility.

And then he saw Tony Perelli, standing over a form lying right in front of the entrance to the house. Silvio and Maria Elena were beside him, and he was holding her, comforting her, and he could hear her weeping.

He moved up slowly and saw the shooter, automatic weapon by his side, two exit wounds in his chest. Silvio looked at Mike and shrugged.

"I made a call."

"He was concentrating on you. I came up behind him. That was it," Tony said.

"You are crazy old men," said Mike. "God bless you both. Is she okay?"

"Just shook up. She's all right."

"Pack what you can. We're getting out of here now."

"You'll get no argument from me," said Silvio. "Come on, honey. Let's get your things."

Maria Elena took one more look at the body lying on the ground and then at Mike, and he knew she had been changed. Even on the edge, she had been in a gun fight and saw death up close. It would be with her for the rest of her life, but at least she had her life, and right now, that was the only thing that concerned him.

"You coming, Tony?"

"No . . . I'm parked down the road, out of sight. It's best if I stay invisible. Silvio knows how to get me if you need me again."

Mike put his hand on his shoulder.

"Thank you, Tony. You're a good man."

Tony started walking away.

"Not as good as you might think, but Silvio is my friend, and we do what we do."

THE SERGEANT MAJOR

CHAPTER 35

Just as Mike was turning to follow them into the house, he saw lights moving down the road.

"*Shit, here comes the all-out assault*," he thought, telling Silvio, who had stopped, "Get her inside and get down . . . and give me your gun!"

Silvio handed it off to him and hurried inside with Maria Elena as Mike got low again, waiting for what was to come. He saw Tony running back to the house, taking a position on the other corner.

Three vehicles pulled into the yard in front of Silvio's house. A man in jeans and a work shirt got out, his hands in the air.

"Don't shoot!"

Mike rose slightly from his prone position.

"Why not?"

"We're the good guys."

"Says who?"

"Says Sergeant Major Steve Kittner, Navy SEALS."

Mike got up, still holding his gun at the ready, and moved toward Kittner.

"I.D.?"

"Come on, Mr. Lang, you know how this works. Let me tell you this. I talked to a friend of yours, a Mr. Walsh. They beat us to the lab. Cleaned out. Not a thing left. No body. No test tubes. No vials. No anything. Just a really cold room."

"Shit!" said Mike.

"Yeah, I know how it feels. Everybody all right here?"

"Yeah."

"You might want to put that gun down now, then."

"Sorry," said Mike, shaking his outstretched hand.

"Walsh thought given what you did, which as I understand it was destroying a whole batch of biological weapons, the bad guys might be after you and you might need a little help . . . but," he said looking down at the body, "I see you've taken care of things."

"Actually, it was the old man," said Mike, looking toward where Tony had been, but he had vanished into the night.

"Good for him. Who all have you got in there?"

"Silvio Caroselli and a young girl named Maria Elena Taylor. Can you get them to Gitmo?"

"That's the plan. My orders are to take you, too."

"Orders from who?"

"Former President of the United States, Jordan Fletcher."

"Well, you're going to have to disobey, 'cause I'm not going. I've got things to do."

"Mr. Lang, I think I know what's going on here. I know about Mr. Sullivan. I think I know why you're here. How about you let us help you this time around . . . at least with the preliminaries?"

Mike looked at him and thought about what he should do next. His mind went back to a warehouse and a young girl tied to a chair.

"You'll do it my way?"

"Yeah, unless you're going to get us all killed . . . then I might have to say something."

"Sounds reasonable," said Mike. "And you'll leave when I tell you to?"

"Absolutely . . . long as no one else," he said, looking at the house, "is in harm's way. It's your ballgame."

"Then I accept," said Mike, again shaking his hand.

"Good. Contrary to what I've been told, you *are* a reasonable man."

"At least you've been talking to people that know me," he said, and laughed.

"Listen, how about I get these two safe and sound at the base. You come along for the ride, and we'll decide what we're going to do, and we'll go from there."

"Sergeant Major, we're all yours. Now, let's get the hell out of here."

THE GITANA

CHAPTER 36

Sergeant Major Kittner deployed some of his men to bag the body, retrieve weapons, and anything else found useful from the sniper's nest and to lock down Silvio's house. They were also instructed to stand guard until daylight, while Kittner and the other members of his team drove back down the road from where they had come to a deserted field where a Seahawk awaited them to lift off and fly to Leeward Point Field at U.S. Naval Station Guantanamo.

Mike looked at those around him. Maria Elena was still clinging to Silvio, and he felt guilt and remorse for the situation in which they found themselves. He said a silent "thank you" to Tony Perelli for getting there in time.

CHAPTER 37

The Seahawk could cruise at approximately 150 miles per hour and after a successful liftoff, covered the 525 miles to the naval base in about 3½ hours. The flight went smoothly, and after landing at Leeward Point Field, the group entered waiting vehicles and were driven past barracks, a school, and even the base's own McDonald's on their way to Joint Task Force Command.

All had been quiet during the flight. Silvio and Maria Elena fell asleep against each other, exhausted after the harrowing night they had experienced. Mike and Kittner spent the flight discussing how to proceed against their common enemy.

When they arrived at headquarters, they were billeted, and were provided clothing and personal supplies to be used during their stay. All of the fatigues were not made to measure. They served their purpose by being clean and comfortable.

After showering, a hot breakfast was provided and helped relieve the tension and weariness they all felt after what they had endured the previous night.

CHAPTER 38

After they had eaten, Kittner took them to a large conference room, which was some type of command center with technical equipment, and introduced them to Base Commander Captain Terrance Potter.

"Mr. Lang . . . Mr. Caroselli . . . Miss Taylor . . . welcome to U.S. Naval Station Guantanamo. Sergeant Major Kittner has provided me with sufficient evidence to indicate there is a potential terroristic threat on this island, which, under the current treaty, allows for direct U.S. intervention. Therefore, I have detailed him to provide protection for you and also take the necessary action to bring this threat to a conclusion.

I want you to understand, Mr. Lang, that you are a civilian and not here on behalf of the United States government. The treaty allows little leeway for direct actions by persons such as yourself.

Having said that, we all understand the situation with Mr. Sullivan, and we wish him a full recovery . . . and you can expect certain latitudes with the Sergeant Major as to how his tactical decisions are carried out. Do I make myself clear?"

"You certainly do, sir," said Mike, extending his hand, "and I appreciate it."

After shaking his hand, the Captain took Mike aside.

"Not so long ago, Mr. Lang, there was a Commander here who lost his position due to some improper activities with civilian contractors. I would like your assurances that I will not follow in his footsteps."

"Captain, I came here for a certain purpose, and that purpose has been discussed with the Sergeant Major, and I think we have arrived at a mutually agreeable plan to achieve it."

The Captain laughed.

"Well, Mr. Lang, that sounds like a bunch of Congressional bullshit! But I'll take it for now, just so we understand each other."

"Understood," said Mike.

Captain Potter nodded and called out, "Sergeant Major Kittner! This group is all yours."

"Aye, aye, sir," replied Kittner.

Mike walked over to him.

"I'm not sure what assurances we just exchanged with each other, but you know that I'm going to do what I have to."

"So does he . . . and more importantly, so do I. Now, let's figure out how we're going to do it."

CHAPTER 39

Everyone took seats around the conference table and Kittner explained the situation.

"You have to understand the Captain, being the Base Commander, has to take the politics of the situation into consideration. Anti-treaty sentiment in Cuba is growing daily. The United States is being accused of bringing back the days of 'banana republics', so in this scenario, we have to be cautious and somewhat secretive in what we do . . . for your protection, the protection of my men, and to ensure that simmering situation doesn't blow up in our faces."

"What exactly does that mean?" asked Mike.

"It means we can't throw a net out there and see what we catch. We can't conduct public searches. We can't go to the media and announce who we are hunting. We have to quietly find the person or persons of interest and deal with them in such a way that any threat they pose is removed without the general public knowing about it."

Mike sat back in his chair.

"Now I know why he called it Congressional bullshit."

"There you have it," said Kittner.

And just then, Mike's encrypted phone pinged.

CHAPTER 40

"Mr. Lang, it's Sam Walsh."

"Hold on. I'm going to put you on speaker and video. I hope you have something for me."

"Indeed I do, Mr. Lang. I have hit the mother load."

"Before you start, Sam, thank you for getting the troops out. I thought Fletcher had hit a wall."

"You know him," said Walsh. "He decided to go through it."

Walsh's face came on the screen and all could see him and hear him over the speaker system.

"This is going to take some time, so bear with me. First of all, the fingerprints on the letter you sent me are a match to prints we recovered in Montana from the helicopter parts and from the Casa Marina in Key West. Anthony Ritzo is definitely Antonio Ortiz," he told Mike. "You have to admit, the guy has a sense of humor."

"What are you talking about?"

"The names. One is the anagram of the other. Antonio is Spanish for Anthony . . . and Ritzo is just Ortiz, scrambled."

"Shit," said Mike. "I missed it completely. Jake would have seen this right away."

"Don't beat yourself up, Mr. Lang," said Sam. "It takes a special type of thought pattern to play around with anagrams, word puzzles, and things like that. His brain just works differently."

"I'm not sure if that is an insult or not, but go on," said Mike.

"No, I didn't mean . . ."

"It's all right, Sam. Get on with it. And Silvio, you can stop chuckling."

And Silvio tried to stop himself, but the dialogue had even brought a smile to Maria Elena.

"The strange thing is, the fingerprints also belong to a young man who was arrested in 1968 when he was 15 in a western Cuban town called Guane. His name is Ferka Bersala."

Silvio, who had been trying to compose himself, sat bolt upright, crossed himself, and shouted, "Madre de Dio! . . . . . Gitana!"

"Silvio, what the hell are you talking about?" asked Mike.

And Maria Elena spoke up.

"Gypsies."

CHAPTER 41

"I recognize the name. He was one of the Gitana . . . the gypsies . . . the Romani . . . that's what they are called here in Cuba. We used him and others for petty rackets . . . running numbers and such."

"It couldn't be him," said Kittner. "He was fifteen in 1968."

"It was probably his father," said Maria Elena. "Many Gitana named their children after the parents."

"Mr. Walsh," asked Silvio, "did you find anything out about a mine in Cabo Corrientes on the Guanahacabibes Peninsula?"

"How did you know that?" asked Walsh. "There was a claim filed in 1966 under the same name."

Silvio pressed his hand to his lower forehead.

"What is it, Silvio?" asked Mike.

"I think I know how this monster may have come to be."

CHAPTER 42

Mike got up and walked over to Silvio.

"Take your time, Silvio. Take your time and tell us."

"You have to understand," began Silvio, "the Gitana have always been part of this culture. European countries drove them out and sent them to the Caribbean to work the sugar cane fields as indentured servants, as slaves, and they settled in many of these islands, including Cuba. But during the Spanish Civil War, they were severely persecuted by Franco, and many of them fled . . . so many that the people here revolted at the influx and a law was passed in 1936 banning them from ever entering the island . . . but many came anyway. Getting into Cuba wasn't the problem. Mr. Lansky told me all of this, as he was not adverse to using them when he felt it necessary.

In the early '60s, a story came out of the western part of the island, where there was a large concentration of Gitana camps, that a gypsy had found the Mérida Treasure. It created quite an uproar in that part of the island and there were riots. Castro sent in troops to quell the disturbance, and the Gitana were forcibly removed and any claims filed were declared illegal. The Gitana fought back, but to no avail. It was at that time that I heard that Bersala had been the man who allegedly found the treasure, and it was said he was killed during the rioting."

"That explains a lot," said Walsh. "The son has it in for those who destroyed his father."

"How better to do it than gain control of a new criminal enterprise?" asked Mike. "To become the man who climbed the ranks of Group 45."

"But," said Kittner, "he can't succeed, because he's Gitana."

"So," said Mike, "he reinvents himself into Antonio Ortiz . . . the alleged son of one of Group 45's assassins."

"And then," said Walsh, "he legitimizes himself as Anthony Ritzo."

"Bersala . . . Ortiz . . . Ritzo . . . they're all the same man," said Mike.

"And here's the clincher . . . and my apologies to you, Mr. Lang . . . Miss Taylor," said Walsh, "what is Spanish for forty-five?"

"Cuarenty cinco."

"Don't tell me," said Mike, "so Grupo Cuarecin is . . ."

And Silvio finished his thought.

"Group 45."

CHAPTER 43

Mike got up and pounded the table.

"Right in front of me again! I missed it! Like I said . . . Jake would have seen it right away. And I know, I know," he said to Walsh, looking at the screen, "my brain works differently. Do you have anything else?"

"Yes. Other than those photos you took, there are no current photos of this guy, but there was a mug shot from the arrest when he was fifteen. Using aging techniques on the recognition software and aging the mug shot, I got a ninety percent match that they are the same man."

"Did you have any luck with what I asked you?" asked Mike.

"Yes," said Walsh, "and I think you are on the right track."

"What did you find?"

"It appears that there was a prominent Havana plastic surgeon who went missing a couple of months ago. His body was then found in an alley behind some bar in Havana, and the police wrote it up as a mugging. His wallet was missing . . . rings, a watch, all his valuables . . . and the guy's blood alcohol was through the roof."

"What aren't you saying?" asked Kittner.

"Well, if you would have the opportunity to read the actual notes that comprise the police report, you'd find that the guy's wife swears that he was a recovering alcoholic who hadn't had a drink in years, and you would also find that he was allegedly spotted getting on an elevator at a certain children's hospital we're all familiar with. It seems that someone who had gone to med school with him saw him entering the elevator and went up to say hello, and the good doctor ignored him and closed the elevator doors. He was described by this former classmate as looking terrified."

"So what's all this mean?" asked Kittner.

"It means Ortiz *did* change his looks," said Mike.

"Seems that way."

Mike looked toward Silvio.

"Now we know, my friend. "We're both after the same man."

"And there's one more thing," said Walsh. "There's an estate on the north shore that, according to the records I found in the local recorder of deeds office, was purchased by a Ferka Bersala a couple of years ago. I found the location, and I was able to run some diagnostics once I did. The place is a fortress. Sensors, cameras, heat signatures showing a small army . . . the works."

"No way in?" asked Kittner.

"Not that I can see. It sits on a cliff. It's a straight drop to the ocean. And at the top of the cliff, there are sensors spaced that would pick up movement coming up and over.

It's gated, walled, and like I said, there are guards everywhere. No flat surfaces to drop to."

"Impregnable, so it appears?" asked Kittner.

"Well, you guys being who you are, I did find a grate on the cliff face for drainage, with a pipe big enough for access that takes you up to the sump room of the basement."

"Now that sounds like an opportunity!" exclaimed Kittner.

"That's all I have," began Walsh, and then he was cut off, his words becoming choppy. Static covered what he was saying, and the video began to break up. "What the . . . hell . . . taking control . . ." and then the video screen came back to life, and there, sitting on a veranda, smoking a cigar, was none other than Anthony Ritzo, a/k/a Antonio Ortiz, a/k/a Ferka Bersala.

CHAPTER 44

"Well, well, Mr. Lang, how are you? Ah, I see Silvio and Maria Elena are with you. Good day to you both. And where is Sergeant Major Kittner? Yes, there he is. Well, enough with the pleasantries. Mr. Lang, you have once again caused me great discomfort. Speaking of which, how is poor Mr. Sullivan doing?"

"Just fine, asshole," said Mike through gritted teeth. "How's the arm?" He saw the anger in Ortiz's eyes, but he ignored Mike's question.

"Not what I have heard, but please, Mr. Lang, the language. There is a lady present. Actually, two of them," and he moved the screen to show an obviously terrified Alicia Taylor sitting in a chair next to him. "Say hello to your sister, my dear."

Maria Elena jumped out of her chair screaming, and Silvio followed, holding her close to him.

"Leave her alone, you monster! Alicia!" and then she began to cry uncontrollably. She heard her sister cry out.

"Maria Elena! Help me!"

"Let her go, Ortiz!" said Mike, rage taking over. "This is between you and me."

Ortiz's pleasant demeanor was gone.

"Indeed it is you I want . . . and you I shall have, Lang. You have meddled in my business for the last time. Midnight tonight. You know where." Then he smiled a grotesque smile. "You don't want to lose another young lady. And if I see Kittner or any of his men anywhere near the sight, your Maria Elena will become an only child," eliciting another scream from her. "Oh shut up, bitch!" sneered Ortiz. "Now who is the asshole, Lang?" and the screen went blank.

CHAPTER 45

Mike fell back into his chair, staring at the blank screen as Walsh came back on.

"What the hell happened?"

"We had a visit from our adversary," said Kittner.

"I'm sorry, Mr. Lang, I don't know how he got in. I'm recalibrating everything here to see where our security failed."

"You won't have any luck," said Silvio, crossing himself. "He's the Devil."

Maria Elena jumped from Silvio's embrace and rushed to Mike and began screaming and pummeling him.

"What have you done?! You have killed her!"

Mike finally got control of her arms and pulled her close to him. He knew he couldn't say anything to comfort her.

Silvio rushed over and pulled her away, glaring at Mike as he did.

"All right. We know the situation. Any thoughts on how to handle it?" asked Kittner, trying to bring the group back into focus.

Mike looked at those around him and remembered his last battle in Havana with the evil of Group 45 and the consequences of that fight. His resolve took over. It was not going to happen again. He looked at Kittner.

"Can you pull up a street map of Havana by the docks? Sam, stay on for a minute, will you?"

"Will do," said Walsh from the screen.

The map soon came up on one of the computer screens on the desk and Mike studied it.

"Sam, can you see this?"

"Yes, I have it pulled up here."

"One of these three buildings – it has a paddle wheel. It was an old rum distillery. We need schematics as to its unguarded points of entry, and I need them now. And I also need the specs and address for that estate on the north shore."

"I'll send you the address, and I'll work on the schematics. Be back as soon as I can," said Walsh, and he was gone.

"Sergeant Major, if Walsh gets you that information about that grate on the cliff face of the estate, do you think you can plan an assault to take place in approximately five hours from now?"

Kittner thought.

"We're pushing it, but yeah, I think we can do it. But how can we? What about the girl?"

"I'm not losing that girl," and he walked over to Marie Elena. "I will bring your sister back to you, I promise you," and she nodded to him through her tears, as Silvio held her hand and then extended his hand to Mike.

"I know you will."

"Silvio, I need you to call Tony, so I can talk to him. There is something I need him to do."

Then Mike looked at Kittner.

"I need to get back to the area near Silvio's house. Can that Seahawk give me another ride?"

"That can be arranged, but what the hell are you up to?"

"I'm going to pay Ortiz a visit. He thinks he's always one step ahead of us. He's secure in the knowledge that he has the trump card – Alicia – and that will determine how we act. I'm not letting him get away with it this time."

"But you can't get in."

"Sure I can," said Mike. "With a little help, I'm going to walk right through the front door."

THE LEADER

CHAPTER 46

Kittner had begrudgingly given Mike what he had asked for, and a Seahawk, pushing it, landed about three hours later with Mike and an ordinance team on board. It had just touched down when a beat up blue pickup came rumbling in from the road, causing the team to take up firing positions.

"Hold up! Hold up!" said Mike. "I asked this guy to come here. He's with me. Everybody take it easy."

Tony Perelli exited the truck after he parked it and walked toward Mike.

"Nice reception you planned for me, Mr. Lang."

"Sorry, Tony. Everybody's just a little on edge."

"Understandable," said Perelli. "Just make sure they know I'm one of the good guys."

"So, how'd you do?"

"Piece of cake. I've got a friend that has a dock right next to that warehouse. We occasionally have need to use his boat, if you know what I mean. So, I told him I needed a little job for the day . . . sort of cleaning up in that area. No problem. Then that geeky guy that works for you . . . that Walsh . . . he's something. He gets into my phone, asks me to wear an earpiece, and he's taking over. So he tells me, vehicle's on the other side of the building. I scoot over to the back of the warehouse, take off a couple of loose boards . . . man, that place is old, by the way, and still smells like rum. I'm inside. Do what we discussed. Back outside. Boom. I'm back on the dock before the car comes around. He had me take a picture. Said he was sending it to you."

Mike took out his phone, held it up, and brought up the picture.

"There it is. Left-hand side, second box from the top."

"How in the hell did you see in there?"

"All I needed was a little pen light. Walsh was giving me directions every step of the way. He said he could see my heat, whatever that means. Anyway, the whiz kid and I pulled it off, no sweat. You're good to go. And now I understand you need to borrow Silvio's truck."

"Yeah, how are you going to get back? I don't want to leave you stranded out here."

"Don't worry. Everything's taken care of. I just gotta walk out to the road, and I'll be good. "You sure you know what you're doin' here?"

"I hope so. I guess we're gonna find out."

"All right. You take care, Mr. Lang. Boys, keep the guns down. I'm leavin'," and Tony turned and headed toward the road.

"Thanks again, Tony. I appreciate it."

"Nothing like a little breaking and entering on a sunny afternoon," said Tony without turning around, and all Mike could do was laugh.

CHAPTER 47

It had only taken the ordinance team a half hour to offload the package in the back of the pickup truck and take care of the electronics, and it was only a half hour later when Mike pulled up to a gate in an elaborate wall on the north shore of the island in the old blue pickup truck with a tarp over the bed.

Two guards appeared as he got out of the truck and approached the gate. They raised their weapons as he spoke.

"Easy, boys. Tell your boss it's just Mike Lang making a social call."

They looked at each other as if in shock, and then one of them went to the gate house and used the intercom. Soon the gate slowly opened, and Mike walked through, putting up his hands to be searched. He only smiled when one of them propelled him toward the main house by jamming the barrel of his weapon into his spine.

"What's your name, friend?" he asked, but he didn't get a response. He just smiled again. "That's okay. I'll remember you."

He walked past more guards through a hallway that ran between rooms, typical rooms of the nouveau riche – a study with books never read, a sitting room where no one sat, and a movie theater where no films were ever played. Finally, he stepped out through French doors onto a veranda overlooking the ocean.

There he came face-to-face with Antonio Ortiz, the leader of Group 45 – the man who had put his friend in a coma. He felt his anger rising, and he fought to control it. That was the key. He had to show that he had the upper hand and he was not concerned about the outcome.

Mike scanned Ortiz's face, moving his head as he looked from one side to the other.

"What are you doing, Lang?"

"I was just checking out your plastic surgery. Not a bad job, especially for a drunk . . . at least that's what the police said. But see, there's one thing you can't change . . . the eyes . . . especially when you're an evil sociopath like you are."

Before Ortiz could even answer, Mike moved over to where Alicia Taylor was still sitting in the chair he had seen her in before, still trembling. Mike held out his hand, and the guard moved to stop him.

"Call off the dogs, Ortiz."

Ortiz smiled and waved the guard away.

"Hello, Alicia. I'm Mike Lang. This gentleman and I have some business to discuss, and then you and I will be leaving."

Ortiz laughed out loud.

"My, my, Mr. Lang! What bravado! Tell me, why don't I just kill you and the girl now and put an end to this comedy of yours?"

Mike opened his closed hand, revealing a small remote with a light blinking green.

"Because that pickup truck next to your gate has a bed loaded with C4, and if I press this little button right here," showing Ortiz, "everything within a hundred yards becomes dust."

Ortiz was momentarily caught off guard.

"And why should I believe you?"

"Don't. Have your men check the bed of the truck, but tell them not to touch the electronics. If they do, it goes boom."

Ortiz nodded to one of his men standing guard on the veranda, and he then moved down the hallway. A short time later, he came back and nodded to Ortiz.

"You're bluffing, Lang," he said. "If you do what you say, you kill yourself and the girl."

"So what. You plan to kill us anyway. This way she lives. Don't worry. I'll still come at midnight," and he moved closer to the tall man. "Just you and me – the end of this."

Mike saw the hatred in Ortiz's eyes, and then he laughed.

"Just like one of your American westerns, huh? The final gun fight on main street. What a fool you are."

"Maybe, but I'm not afraid to die. I know who I am. How about you? Are you some gypsy punk . . . the son of a failed miner . . . or a corporate maker of biological weapons and the killer of children? Or are you just another insane killer – greedy, evil, pathetic, without any care or concern for anyone else? Are you, or any of you, afraid to die?"

Mike could see that Ortiz was in a slowly growing rage. Ortiz tried to calm himself, but to no avail. Mike had struck a nerve.

"My father was murdered by people on this island who thought they were better than he was . . . than we all were . . . the Gitana. He rightfully owned the mine where he and he alone had found the treasure of the Mérida, and he was killed because of it, and his property taken from him. But don't worry, Mr. Lang, I'm in the process of getting it back, and I will. And then I will deal with the people of this island and people like them everywhere. The time will come when I will rule it all, and I will take this organization to heights that no one has ever imagined. And you, Mr. Lang, will not stop me. Your friend, Mr. Sullivan, may live, but it is only existence, not living, and that is because of me. And you will suffer a similar fate. So, the answer to your question is 'no'. I am not afraid to die, because I have no intention of dying, as you will certainly see, as I most happily meet you at midnight tonight."

"Yeah, that's what I thought. Come on, Alicia, we're leaving. See you tonight, asshole. Don't be late."

Again the guard moved toward him. Mike looked at Ortiz, raising the remote.

"Let him go," said Ortiz. "Let him take his little whore with him. Tonight you die, Lang! And then I intend to deal with all your friends."

Mike paused and looked out over the ocean and then smiled at Alicia.

"Nice view, Ortiz. You better enjoy it. You're right about one thing . . . someone will die tonight," and he walked through the French doors with Alicia and headed down the hallway. He could feel her trembling, and he whispered to her, "Just hold on. It's almost over."

They exited the front door and made their way to the open gate and passed through. Mike opened the passenger door of the pickup truck and set Alicia gently inside and whispered to her, "I'll be right back," as he noticed something going on at another entrance to the estate.

He then turned and walked back to where the guard stood, still staring at what he had noticed. When he had gotten close enough to the one who had jabbed him in the spine, he brought up his fist, catching him right below the chin, and the guard crumpled to the ground.

"That's for bad manners," he said.

As the other guard moved toward him, he held up the remote.

"Uh, uh."

Then he walked toward the truck as if he didn't have a care in the world, opened the driver's side door, and pulled away from the estate on the north shore.

THE PLAN

CHAPTER 48

As soon as Mike was on the road heading back toward Silvio's, he was on the phone talking to Kittner.

"We have to call off the raid on the estate."

"Why? My men were flown in and are in position. Did something go wrong with the girl?"

"No, I have her. We're heading back now to Silvio's, and I'll soon have her on the chopper and on her way home"

Kittner had put Mike on speaker, and he could hear Maria Elena and Silvio thanking him in the background.

"I'll be damned," said Kittner, "you actually pulled it off."

"Just like any bully," said Mike, "you have to stand up to them."

"So why no assault?"

"They have biologicals. I saw a truck there. They were unloading metal cases exactly like those I saw at the hospital."

"Makes sense," said Kittner. "Got to figure our boy would want some close by."

"We just have to keep making it up as we go," replied Mike.

"Yeah, I guess so. And you know, there always seems to be some civilian somewhere causing us to do that. Why should you be any different?"

"That's the spirit, Kittner. That's the spirit. Listen, I want to get to Silvio's and get this stuff back in the chopper before I accidentally hit the wrong button on this remote. Call me after you have your plans in place and after Alicia safely arrives. I want to make sure she's safe with her sister before I start figuring out my side of this."

"Will do, and . . . nice work."

"Thanks Kittner. You said that like you actually meant it."

CHAPTER 49

Mike was back at Silvio's, had just washed and heated up some of the pulled pork that was still in the refrigerator from what seemed an eternity ago and was sitting down to eat when his encrypted phone rang. To his surprise, it was Maria Elena and Silvio both joining Kittner on the phone, Silvio speaking first.

"Thank you, Mike, for bringing this beautiful young girl back safely to us. I apologize for my earlier anger."

"Don't worry, Silvio, there was reason to be angry."

And then Maria Elena came on the line.

"I'm sorry for before, Mr. Lang. I should have believed you. Thank you for keeping your promise and bringing my sister back to me."

"You had every right to be upset, and believe me, bringing her back to you was my pleasure."

And then it was Kittner's turn.

"Sorry, I don't have time to pat you on the back, but your friend Walsh did a hell of a job with the schematics for that old dump, and we do have a way in. There is a grate, ocean-side, just above the water line, that leads to a tunnel that leads to a basin for the wheel. We come in scuba gear and come out behind the wheel, check heat signatures for the location of the guards, take them out, and then we take Ortiz."

"So what you're telling me is you need total silence, you can't be seen, and a small splash gives away the whole operation?"

"Pretty much," said Kittner.

"Okay. Sounds good," said Mike. "So, when do you go in?"

"When we know all parties are in position, including you," and he discussed the plan in detail.

"Sounds good to me. So all we can do now is wait?"

"Yes, we wait, and my team runs through the scenarios again and again and again to make sure we have it perfect."

Silvio spoke up.

"I still don't understand why when this Devil gets there with his men you don't just go take them."

"Because I know Ortiz," said Mike. "He's lost Alicia, but he's going to bring something for leverage. I'm not sure what, but I have an idea."

Kittner spoke softly to him.

"You think he will bring some product, don't you?"

"I wouldn't put it past him."

"That makes things a little more dicey."

"Just be prepared for it."

"We'll bring a little extra gear, but what about you?"

"I'll play it by ear and hope for the best."

"Mike, are you sure you're ready for this?" asked Kittner. "If you're right and something goes wrong . . ."

"I'm ready, and your plan is going to work. Just don't make a splash."

"Mike," said Silvio, "be careful. Do what you have to do."

"Don't worry, Silvio. This ends tonight."

CHAPTER 50

The rest of the day was spent on encrypted phones going over various scenarios with Kittner and his team. All were amazed at their attention to detail, but given what they did and where they had to do it, they came to understand why they were the best and their admiration continued to grow with that understanding.

At approximately 10:30 that night, Walsh called Mike and Kittner and reported seven heat signatures at the warehouse. Five were moving in and two were staying outside. Also, he had tapped video cameras on a newer warehouse down at the docks, and he had scanned the perimeter of the building throughout the day. There were ongoing vehicles patrolling the area with men getting out occasionally, men who were armed, walking around the perimeter of the building, and then going inside.

"It's like we suspected," said Mike, "Ortiz isn't taking any chances. That's why you couldn't go in early."

Kittner, who, with his men, had left Gitmo and had taken up position at a staging area near the warehouse, agreed.

"It's just as well," he said. "He'll never see us coming."

"Or hear you," smiled Mike.

"Right."

"Keep your eye on the place for another hour," said Mike, to Kittner.

"Give you enough time to get into position?" Kittner checked his watch. "That's a little close. Why the wait?"

"I want to see if they're still doing any patrols, or if anyone else is coming so we know what we're up against."

The hour passed and Walsh again called them.

"There's nothing . . . just the two heat signatures outside the man door, the two on the upper deck, and then three set up in a shooting triangle that will give them perfect aim at just about where you plan to be standing."

"*Just like last time*," said Mike, to himself. "Well, that makes me feel better, Sam. All right, I'm almost there. Let's do this."

Neither Maria Elena nor Alicia, nor Silvio, had been able to go to sleep. Before Kittner had left, Silvio came up to him.

"Thank you for doing this for these two girls and the other people who live here. This man is a monster, and he needs to be treated as such."

"Understood, Mr. Caroselli," said Kittner, patting him on the shoulder. "We'll do our job."

THE WAREHOUS E

CHAPTER 51

When Mike had pulled out from Silvio's in the blue pickup truck, it all started to come back to him as he hit Highway 222 to the Avenideasta, east from the Siboney District, to the Avenida Carlos Manuel De Cespedes, to the Canal De Entrada, the entrance to Havana Harbor, past the Terminal Sierra Maestra and the ferry terminal to the docks and warehouses beyond.

He was reliving it all again. He could see the old Impala coming close to them with a group of teenage joyriders, who were really Navy SEALS, planting a tracking device on the Mercedes in which he was a passenger. As he pulled up to the warehouse, he could still see Paula sitting in a chair. He could see Matthews pull the trigger. He had to stop. Alicia was safe. It wasn't going to happen again. So far, he had outplayed Ortiz.

His adrenaline began to fill his body with energy, and he tried to calm himself.

He parked the truck, exited, and walked as casually as his emotions would let him to the man door, where he was met by two guards and patted down. One of them opened the door and nodded for him to go in.

The scene was surreal. He could feel himself start to sweat. He was back in time . . . sights, sounds, smells . . . all the same.

The man sitting on the upper deck in a chair beside a table in a silk shirt, linen slacks, and sandals wasn't Ortiz. It was a crippled Benjamin Matthews, and Paula was right beside him. His fists clenched and unclenched, and he fought to keep control.

It was Ortiz who brought him back to reality. Now he fully recognized the man in front of him, took note of the guard at the side, looked to the stack of crates to his left, and the pool with the water wheel to his right. His sense of hearing was now on alert, and he compartmentalized what Ortiz was saying.

"Good evening, Mr. Lang. You have kept your word. Can I interest you in a glass of Anejo Rum? A very special drink here in Cuba. Blanco Rum . . . very, very light . . . is aged in oak barrels for no less than one and no more than three years to give it the darkened color and flavor you see here. Personally, I think two years is perfect, and I have my special blend aged in such a fashion."

"No thanks," said Mike, cutting him off. "I'm sort of particular about who I drink with."

"I see," said Ortiz, setting down the glass and picking up a small silver canister. "Are you as particular about how you die?"

"I've had a lot of people try different methods, but I'm still here."

Ortiz set the canister back on the table and then picked up something else. It appeared to be a portable breathing device. He showed it to Mike and then set it down. He then picked up a Glock and aimed it at Mike.

"You know, Mr. Lang, I was going to offer you a choice. This canister is one of the very few containers I have left since you destroyed most of the biological weapons my team had created. But what I have here is certainly enough to kill you . . . and a good percentage of the city of Havana once I release it into the air. I was going to give you a choice between that and a quick death, but I have to tell you, this matter has become quite personal to me. I think I want to see you suffer, and I want you to know that after you die, I intend to kill many people . . . Silvio, Alicia, Maria Elena, Master Sergeant Kittner, and . . . oh, yes . . . of course . . . Charlotte Kosior."

"I sort of figured you'd try something, you sick piece of shit, so I decided I better not die tonight."

"Really?" said Ortiz.

Mike had not heard a sound . . . not a splash, not a drop, not a foot fall . . . but he saw the slight movement in the shadows behind Ortiz. Then there was a puff and a spray of red as the guard standing at Ortiz's right fell off the platform. Then Sergeant Major Steve Kittner put his silenced weapon to the base of Ortiz's brain.

"Slowly, put the weapon down on the table. You make any movement I don't like, you're dead."

A smile on his face, Ortiz complied.

Kittner then picked up the canister and put it in the sealed pouch he had brought after he and Mike had discussed the possibilities of what Ortiz might do.

Ortiz still smiled.

"I assume my other men are similarly disposed of, Sergeant Major?"

"I would say that's a safe bet," said Kittner. He then prodded Ortiz with his weapon. "Get up. Head down the steps."

Ortiz, still smiling, slowly got to his feet. As he did so, he seemed to stumble and moved his cane to support himself, but the movement became an upward arc as the bottom of the cane flew off, revealing a long silver blade. The arc continued upward and then came down, slashing Kittner's arm, his gun dropping and falling off the upper deck. Ortiz then moved to grab the pouch, but Kittner lashed out with his leg, sending Ortiz stumbling down the first few steps.

Mike had already began to move to his left and turned over one of the crates he had memorized from Tony's photo. He pulled the Glock from its hiding place. Ortiz had righted himself and in a rage, had made it down the steps and was moving toward Mike as quickly as he could, the blade high in the air. Ortiz was almost upon him, and Mike fired. Ortiz stumbled but kept coming, and Mike fired twice more. Ortiz sank to his knees, dropping the blade, his fingers tearing at his shirt and revealing a strange tattoo on the right side of his chest. He then fell forward, his eyes locked in place, as Mike stood over him.

"I told you someone would die tonight."

Kittner was coming down the steps, and his other men were moving toward them.

"Are you all right?" asked Mike.

"Yeah, just a nick," he said, blood dripping from his arm. The cut was long and deep, and Mike looked at him and smiled.

"That's going to need some stitches."

Kittner smiled back and said, "Thanks, mom. Now let's get out of here. The cleanup crew will be coming. By the way, how are you doing?"

"I couldn't be better."

"Well, just in case you were concerned, I want you to know that Sergeant Flynn here had Ortiz in his sights the whole way. If you hadn't managed to get that Glock out from under that crate that you seemed to be fumbling with over there, he would have taken the shot."

"I appreciate it, but I had it under control."

"Yeah, I saw that," he said.

"Is the estate secured?"

"Just as we talked about."

"Nice plan, by the way."

CHAPTER 52

The plan Mike had mentioned had been simple in design, but required detailed execution.

At approximately 11:30 P.M., after receiving notice from Walsh about the location of the heat signatures, Kittner's team had entered the water south of the old rum factory. They had been helicoptered to an abandoned factory sight ten miles away and driven to within one mile of the old docks, where they entered the water and had found the grate Walsh had described. Using underwater torches to cut through the rusted metal proved to be no problem, and they followed the tunnel they found silently until they saw light above them and found the base of the waterwheel. Surfacing slowly, they huddled at the back edge of the wheel and waited.

At 11:57 P.M., Walsh notified them that Mike had entered and gave them the final position of the guards. Slowly and gently, they pulled themselves out of the water, one by one, and faded into the shadows, each man stalking their particular prey.

At the same time, on Kittner's orders, an assault began at the estate on the north shore. Because of Ortiz's hack of the system when he made his on-screen appearance at the command center, he had allowed Walsh to hack into *his* system, and Walsh was able to neutralize all communications and the sensors on the cliff face, which Kittner's team scaled without difficulty and came onto the veranda, which was unguarded due to Ortiz's absence. They made short work of the guards that remained and were already in the process of taking control of the biological weapons that had been brought there, as well as taking all computers, hard drives, and anything else that could prove useful in providing information about Group 45 and Ortiz's plans.

In reply to Mike's complement, Kittner responded, "Sometimes they work out. All depends who's on your side. I know I'm not Jake Sullivan, but . . ."

"Please, don't even go there. If he knew you said that, I'd never hear the end of it." And then the reality of Jake's situation came to them both, and they left the warehouse in silence.

EPILOGUE

CHAPTER 53

They were all on the tarmac at Leeward where the plane that would take Mike to Miami was waiting -- Silvio, Maria Elena, Alicia, Tony, and Kittner. There were hugs and handshakes all around, except for the Sergeant Major, whose right arm was in a sling.

His team and the Federales were rounding up the rest of Ortiz's crew.

"So far, every one of them has this tattoo," said Kittner.

"Does it mean anything to you?" Mike asked as he extended a photo to Silvio.

Silvio looked at it and handed it back to Mike, crossing himself as he did so.

"Gitana symbol – The Horned God."

Alicia spoke up.

"You must be careful, Mr. Lang. As part of my environmental courses, I studied Paganism – the age old relationship between man and nature. The Horned God is a symbol of many things. Primarily, it's a duality. Summer – winter . . . day – night . . . good – evil . . . life – death. Those who claim this symbol as their own believe they have those powers, they control those elements, and they are very, very dangerous."

"You have to understand, Mike, these men are all part of his gypsy family. I think the evil man you killed went back to his roots. You must be very careful. You've started a blood feud now with his Gitana family. They will stop at nothing to bring about your end," said Silvio.

Mike laughed it off.

"Sounds like just another day at the office," and he reached out and hugged Silvio.

"Be serious about this, Mike. Be careful."

"I will, Silvio . . . I will. And you take care of this island and your hospital."

"Thank you for restoring the memory of my child."

"Silvio, we both know nothing could lessen that memory. You take special care, my friend."

"And your friend, Mr. Sullivan, Mike . . . he will recover. I know this to be true."

Mike could only nod. He shook Kittner's extended left hand, gave Alicia and Maria Elena one last hug, and then turned and walked to the waiting plane.

THE PATIENT

CHAPTER 54

When Mike arrived in Miami, he went straight to the hospital. He knew Charlie had come down again to spend time with Linda, Jennifer, and Jessica as they visited Jake, and he found them in his room. They all hugged and talked and laughed, and as Mike looked at his friend, he could tell no difference in his condition, but Linda and the girls filled him in on movements they had seen and other signs that they believed showed improvement. While he hoped that they were right, he had his doubts.

Finally, they left and only Charlie remained.

"Thank you, Mike," she said.

"For what?"

"For keeping your promise to me and coming home."

"I'll always come home to you. I keep telling you that."

"And I keep worrying you won't."

Mike looked over at Jake.

"Do you mind if I stay a little longer?"

"No," she said. "Tell him what you did. He would want to know." She kissed him and squeezed his hand, and then she left.

Mike pulled up a chair and sat down beside Jake's bed and looked at his friend.

"All right, Sullivan, this has to stop. I could have used you down there. There were these clues I missed, and you would have figured them out . . . not that you're smarter than me. Our brains just work differently. This is just like you. I'm working my tail off and you keep resting. Come on, enough is enough. Come on, Jake."

Then Mike grabbed his hand and squeezed and turned to leave, and then looked back.

"I got him, Jake. I got him. You should have seen Silvio and everyone else. You would have been proud of them. But we have a problem. We're fighting a family of gypsies, and they have a biological weapon they are going to use on Key West. I know, it sounds crazy. It's a long story, and I'll tell you about it later. The bad guys keep coming, Jake. You have to get out of that bed, 'cause we have to stop them."

CHAPTER 55

The nurse on the late night shift was giving meds and taking vitals. She went into room 413 and checked on the patient. Poor man. He had been like this so long. What a shame.

It scared her to death when he opened his eyes and asked, "Where did Mike go?"

COMING

FALL 2019

GYPSIES IN THE PALACE
CHIP BELL

CHIP BELL

1725 FIFTH AVENUE
ARNOLD, PA 15068

724-339-2355

chip.bell.author@gmail.com
clb.bcymlaw@verizon.net
www.ChipBellAuthor.com

FOLLOW ME ON FACEBOOK
facebook.com/chipbellauthor

FOLLOW ME ON TWITTER
@ChipBellAuthor

FOLLOW ME ON PINTEREST
pinterest.com/chipbellauthor
/the-jake-sullivan-series

TAKE THE TIME TO REVIEW
THIS BOOK ON AMAZON
amazon.com/author
/chipbellauthor.com

Made in the USA
Lexington, KY
25 April 2019